Mahmud Khan was born in India, brought up in Pakistan, and now lives in England with his family. He is a lover of humour, logic, mathematics, science and philosophy.

He is the author of
Kuch Gunjoan Ki Shaan Mein
a book of humour in Urdu

The Logic of Half a Moustache

Mahmud Khan

Published in 2010 by YouWriteOn.com

First Edition

Illustrations by Mahmud Khan

ISBN-10: 1849232121
ISBN-13: 978-1849232128

www.mahmudkhan.com

Published by YouWriteOn.com

For

Mahboob, Rukhshanda, Rushda,
Sara, Rehan

and

in loving memory of the late

Chacha Punnu Khan

Contents

"Are you riding a camel?"
"Why do you ask? Can't you see for yourself?"
"There's no harm in asking, is there?"

Preface

The Universe is a very mysterious place! It was smaller than a dot at the time of the Big Bang, some fifteen billion years ago. It is made from only a handful of different types of particles, which are governed by a few fundamental forces. Yet look at its diversity now, its immensity, and the fact that it gives rise to life. What a mystery this is, that some parts of the Universe have become alive and self-aware! And that the Universe can reflect about itself, write about itself and read about itself – as does that portion of the Universe which is you, right now.

No one can think on these matters without bewilderment, and along with our bewilderment goes a desire for an explanation. But the nature of explanation itself is a bewildering matter, and there seems to be no end to our need for it. Indeed, any explanation seems likely to give rise to a host of other matters which need to be explained. And we, who seek to explain, are ourselves an unexplained mystery.

We are first and foremost human beings who interact with one another, and in my experience this interaction can be just as confusing as the rest of the cosmos! The cultural differences which are so often a very powerful source of this confusion can also give rise to something else: conflict. I know this first hand. I was born in India just before Partition – the division of the Indian subcontinent into the Hindu state of India and the

Islamic state of Pakistan – and I witnessed the ongoing hostility that this caused.

Although confusion can give rise to conflict, it can also give rise to something less unpleasant. It has always amazed me how features taken for granted in one culture can seem humorous or even absurd from the point of view of another. Since making my permanent home in Britain, this has become more obvious than ever. Many of the stories herein are based on real-life episodes highlighting these differences.

I believe it is sometimes important to look at things from a new perspective, to highlight unfamiliar aspects of life. To illustrate my point, just bend down and look back through your legs. A familiar scene will be dramatically transformed in ways which cannot be appreciated without such an experiment!

Following the Socratic tradition, lots of questions have been asked in this book, but very few of these have been answered. Answering questions is of course much more difficult!

I believe there is something here for everyone. I hope you will find the written sketches of life, culture and the Universe to be intriguing, and maybe sometimes more than a little bizarre – rather like the face of a man with half a moustache!

I am highly indebted to my good friend Richard Hall, who has collaborated with me throughout the writing and production of this book, and provided invaluable help and advice. Any errors that might still be found in the book are entirely his responsibility.

Mahmud Khan
Bradford, England, 2010

www.mahmudkhan.com

Asian Perspectives

Asian Perspectives

Velcome to England

I had always had a vision of England as a place of learning, and of her people as being among the most civilised in the world, an idealised vision derived from English films and the reports of returning visitors. I imagined very clean streets, all the people well-groomed and wearing suits or skirts, and using perfumes which I could almost smell. They were definitely not burdened with luggage, except for the occasional folded umbrella.

To some extent this vision was my reason for coming to England to study in 1971. It was reinforced on the plane, when the English passenger sitting next to me and occupying the window seat realised that I was trying to look out at the Alps, and very kindly gave up his seat for me to drink in the views to my heart's content, leaving me with the whole of the double seat for myself.

I thought my English was reasonably good when I set off. I managed to understand people quite comfortably at the airports and on the plane. However, as soon as I came out of Heathrow Airport, and was in England, I could neither understand nor could I be understood by the local people. This was partly due to the speed and the dialect of the speech I encountered, but also to the fact that the pronunciation I had learned in Pakistan was not always correct. However, I was still feeling buoyant as I travelled to King's Cross station.

At King's Cross I was confused by the layout of such a huge station and asked directions from a casually dressed man who was sitting on the ground and seemingly not busy. I told him I had just arrived from Pakistan, was a new student, and wanted to go to Bradford. He obliged by taking me all the way to the right platform, where my train was ready to leave.

I was very impressed by the hospitality he displayed, which more than confirmed my expectations of the English. However, when I was about to get on the train, he asked for some money, and I had to tell him that I had no spare cash on me. He was seemingly unaffected by my inability to pay him, for he stayed to see me off, giving what I took to be a goodwill gesture, by moving his right hand up and down with two fingers raised to make a 'V'. English people seemed to me to be even more magnanimous in their hospitality than I had expected.

While I was reciprocating his goodwill gesture, and settling down in my window seat, the train started moving out of the station. As he receded from view, we both continued to gesture to each other in the same friendly manner.

The British Raj

The British occupation of India between 1858 and 1947 is known as the British Raj. My father would tell me the following story about the Raj:

> *When the English took over our countries, they wanted to fix the wages. They didn't know how to fix the wages of their own people in relation to those of the Indian natives.*
>
> *So they devised a secret experiment. They gave an equal amount of money to an English person and an Indian person chosen at random, and asked them both to go to town and enjoy themselves.*
>
> *In the evening, when they came back, their pockets were checked: the Indian pocket was almost as full as before, but the English pocket was empty. These experimental results were taken to reflect the relative needs of Indian and English workers, and wages were fixed accordingly.*

Praise but no raise

A friend of mine, Mr Hussain, a graduate from Pakistan, once gave me an account of a sad experience at the hands of the English. After coming to England, he worked in a local government department, and the experience he told me about had left him very disenchanted with his employers.

According to Hussain, his English employers had always given him the impression that his English was good, and they had not criticised it in any way. "Don't worry, Mr Hussain," they would say, "I can understand you perfectly." It had gone on like this until the day Hussain applied for promotion to a managerial position in the same department. The same people who had previously encouraged him to believe his English was *good* now turned down his application on the basis that his English was *poor*. “Mr Hussain,” he was told, “I’m afraid your communication skills are not adequate for the position.”

Hussain immediately concluded that they were making an excuse for not giving him the promotion, and that he was a victim of institutional racism. This conclusion was supported when a white candidate was appointed to the position.

It was not possible to convince him that the earlier positive remarks about his English had been well-intentioned and had arisen from politeness and a desire to encourage him; but that when he applied for promotion he had to be presented with the bitter truth.

Originally, I’m sure, Hussain’s employers had simply not wanted to hurt his feelings. It is a great cultural difference between England and Pakistan that in England people are much less inclined to point out the faults of others. If Hussain had been aware of this fact he might have learned to take praise with a degree of scepticism.

The new student at Leeds

When I came to England to study, my first desire on arriving in Bradford was to see my new university, the University of Leeds. I was excited about discovering the nature of these famed British universities, and to learn my way around my own, before my Mathematics course began.

While still in Pakistan, I had received a great deal of correspondence from the University. This was mainly from the School of Mathematics, but my letter of admission was from the Deputy Registrar, one of the senior members of the University. With these papers in my pocket, I set off for Leeds.

When I arrived, I took out my admission letter and set about tracking down this Deputy Registrar. It seemed important to me that I present myself to him as soon as possible, and I was very keen to make a good impression.

The University was a huge place and I quickly found myself lost. Eventually, when I had plucked up enough courage, I approached a man who looked fairly official, and asked, in my best English, "Vhere is Dipty Register, please?"

But the man failed to understand my question and asked me to repeat it. Realising I had mispronounced 'Deputy Registrar', I gave my next best attempt, but still couldn't pronounce the magic words. I went through various increasingly wild approximations, like "Depty Register", "Dipity Register" and "Dipewty Registeror" but, to my dismay, none of these options was found acceptable. In the end I gave up and held out my letter, pointing to the relevant spot.

At long last I found myself in the Deputy Registrar's Office, but was unable to persuade the member of staff there to let me see the man in person. When I showed my various letters to her, she told me that I had come to the wrong place altogether. I should have gone to the School of Mathematics, about half a mile in the opposite direction.

Success for Jehovah's Witnesses

Jehovah's Witnesses are always willing to devote much time to their missionary work. Whenever they knock on our door, we now politely decline to discuss religious matters with them, because I have found that once you show any interest in their subject-matter, they become disinclined to let you go back indoors. And when they do eventually release you, they give you homework in the form of reading to be completed before their next visit.

We once had an Asian lady living next-door, called Chachi Daro, a very intelligent lady. She was a strict traditional Muslim. We could hardly believe it when we noticed that she had started to welcome Jehovah's Witnesses regularly into her home, particularly as we knew she couldn't speak English very well. Each day, they left the house very happy and Chachi Daro too was looking more and more satisfied.

One day my wife, who could not contain herself any longer, asked her about this mystifying state of affairs.

"What on Earth's the matter? You're not converting to Christianity, are you?"

"No, no, nothing like that," she replied sweetly. "I'm only trying to improve my English."

It's time I spoke English

English grammar can cause paradoxical results when sentences are translated literally into Urdu. Here are just four curious examples of the sort of thing I have in mind:

- It's very cold. ***I*** should wear a coat when ***you*** go out.
- ***I*** shouldn't stay up too late. ***You'll*** be tired tomorrow.
- It's time I ***went*** home.
- I'd rather you ***cooked*** the dinner ***now***.

The value of books

In Pakistan, our parents had to buy our school books for us. Some of our classmates would play truant and sell their school books to make extra pocket money for cigarettes, cinema, and other addictive needs. The good boys (of whom I was one) thought it was terrible to do this.

"They are very bad boys," our parents would tell us. "They need their books for their schooling. They shouldn't throw away their parents' hard-earned money. Without education they'll never make anything of themselves. Poverty and hunger – that's all they'll have to look forward to."

But things don't always turn out the way you expect. We were much scandalised when we later discovered that some of these boys actually benefited from their earlier experience, by going on to become some of the most successful booksellers in the region. Moreover, many of us good boys went to work in their bookstores!

The logic of half a moustache

Sheikhu, one of my acquaintances, and a barber by trade, used to keep an exceptionally long, shining black, magnificent and twirling moustache – a feature noticeable from a long distance, and a source of great pride and joy to its owner.

However, when I bumped into Sheikhu one day, I noticed that his pride and joy had been interfered with so seriously that I had my doubts about his sanity. I could hardly contain my laughter at his strange and bizarre appearance: he had shaven off *half* of what was his most distinguishing feature!

"What have you done to yourself?" I asked in puzzlement, while still trying not to laugh. Sheikhu sighed, and proceeded to unravel the enigma.

"As much as I loved my moustache," he sighed, "I was fed up with the endless taunts from the local kids. *'Sheikhu, Sheikhu,'* they'd call, *'it's not fancy-dress tonight, didn't you know?'* Or, *'Meow, meow, Sheikhu, why do you have whiskers like a cat?'* Wherever I went, they had some new joke at my expense.

"So, in the end, I decided to shave it off. But I was apprehensive about such a drastic change, and I decided to test the water first by shaving off just half. If shaving off half the moustache didn't have any unpleasant consequences, then I could go on and shave off the rest."

"You've clearly given this matter your thorough consideration," I politely remarked.

"Oh yes, Khan Saab!" he responded ponderously. "But, alas, as I feared, the teasing has only worsened! It used to be just the kids – now I'm the laughing stock of the whole neighbourhood! I'm really glad I was cautious. If shaving off half the moustache makes things worse, the only logical conclusion is that shaving it all off would make things unbearable. Thank God for my sanity."

Aren't we all Sheikhus in our own ways?

My marriage: a bold proposal

In any culture, baldness may create some difficulties in the way of getting married; but the difficulties are even more pronounced in Asian cultures, since baldness is more frowned upon in Asia than in Europe, and is inclined to provoke very disparaging remarks. In Pakistan, I have known the bare-headed to be treated like the bare-footed beggars of the street! No wonder we don't see any bald Indian film heroes.

When, at the age of only fifteen, I started to go bald, my self-esteem was badly shaken. It seemed as though with the loss of my crowning glory, I would lose all chance of romance in my life. It was a most traumatic experience. It should not be surprising that there is a great deal of quackery and charlatanism associated with baldness, which feed on young people's desperation. My parents were greatly concerned. And this concern increased as, over the next few years, my head became more and more unsightly.

Eventually my mother took me to the local shrine of Golra Sharif, where there were many sacred stones, which the pilgrims used against their various ailments. I picked one up and rubbed it on my head as advised by Mother. Where else on human bodies these stones might already have been used, only God knows! I could only guess by their being so smooth and oily from constant use. In my case, I suspect that rubbing the stone on my head actually left me with *fewer* hairs.

The awful balding process continued unabated, despite the various desperate measures of which my head was the innocent victim. Indeed my head eventually became, in all respects other than size, not unlike one of the Golra Sharif stones themselves!

Mother knew it would be very hard to get anyone married with a head like mine. But she eventually plucked up the courage to take me all the way from Rawalpindi to her sister's home in Gujrat, to discuss the possibility of my marrying her daughter Rukhsana. My elder sister came with us to lend moral support.

My uncle, whose consent was essential, hadn't seen me since I was a boy, and he was appalled by what had become of me. As soon as he saw me, he shook his head and exclaimed with horror and disappointment: "What on earth have you done to your head?" I was stunned by what I took to be an insult. Obviously, Mother had expected him to be concerned, and she said: "Don't worry. It's only a matter of a few more visits to Golra Sharif. His hair will grow in time." But Uncle's scepticism showed on his face. For him, seeing was believing.

Mother then tried a light-hearted approach. "Well," she said, "in the meantime, you can just think of him as having a rather high forehead." Uncle didn't think it was funny.

My sister then chipped in: "Oh, no. Foreheads don't go all the way to the back. You'll just have to think of his eyes as being set a bit lower than normal." But my sister was no more successful than Mother had been.

Even Aunty tried to rescue my self-esteem, and said: "I can't see anything wrong with him except that his hair is parted down the middle. It's just that the parting is a bit too wide, that's all!"

But Uncle was unmoved by all this, and the visit eventually turned out to be unsuccessful. Throughout the whole proceedings, I simply sat as a silent spectator; I could not even muster up enough courage to make eye contact with Uncle. We returned to Rawalpindi greatly disappointed.

On the way home, I felt very embarrassed, demoralised and dejected. While I was complaining to God about His putting such uncles in charge of beautiful young women, Mother's remark, *'his hair will grow in time'*, kept ringing in my mind, and eventually raised a glimmer of hope in my heart: within a few days of our arrival back home, I bought myself a hairpiece!

The following month, we went back to Gujrat for a second attempt – this time not as beggars but as choosers!

Uncle was from simple village folk, and for him seeing was believing. And what he saw, when I walked in, was nothing short of a miracle: Mother's faith in the sacred stones had been vindicated. In fact, my newly-grown, luxuriant hair looked, if anything, rather better than his own, and this time it was Uncle who found it difficult to make eye contact with me. Mother sat there proudly, and did not have to do any advocacy on my behalf at all. She simply said to Uncle: "You see, I told you." When he had recovered, Uncle gave the marriage his wholehearted support.

Ironically, I soon found that the whole charade had been of no importance to Rukhsana, who turned out to have been upset by her father's original rejection of me. We have been happily married ever since.

Bollywood justice

Indian films, sometimes referred to as 'Bollywood' films, are a truly fantastic form of entertainment. To give you just one example of what I mean, there has always been a great distinction, in action scenes, between the villain's bullet and the hero's. The villain's bullet is always untrained, and finds it very difficult to catch up with the hero. Even if it does, the hero will easily dodge it without even having to look behind. The hero's bullet, on the other hand, is trained in warfare; it perseveres and does not give up its pursuit; it seeks out the villain even if it has to negotiate corners!

The lion's share

I once went with my wife to the new multiplex cinema in Bradford to see an Indian movie, featuring that most famous of Indian actors, Amitabh Bachchan, in a supporting role. It being a Wednesday, we only had to pay the reduced rate of £7 for the two of us.

We were quite late when we entered the cinema. It was pitch dark, and the film was just about to start. A notice was on the screen with the following request: '*For the consideration of others around you, please switch off your mobile phones*'. We very quietly felt our way to two seats near the entrance door, so as not to disturb anyone.

An hour and a half later there was an intermission during the film, and the lights were switched on. We were taken aback to discover that we were in fact the only two people in the whole place!

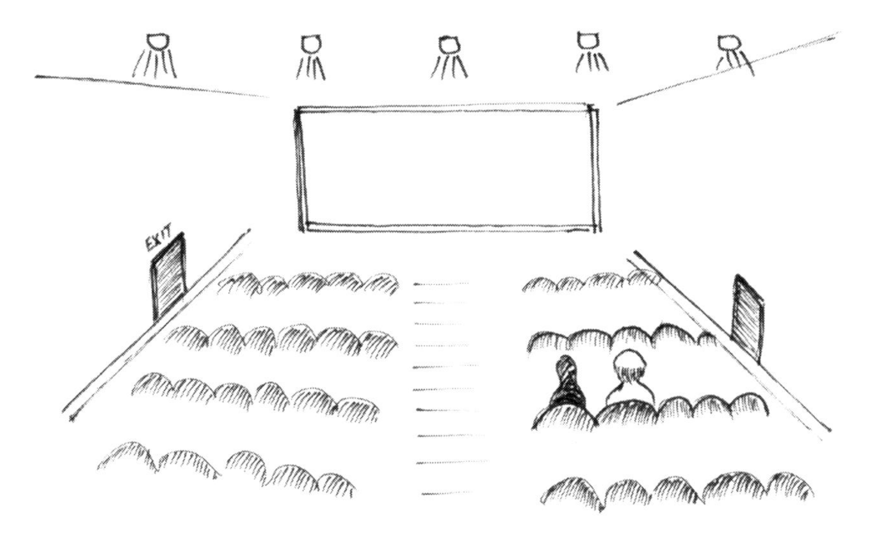

I never use a mobile, but Rukhsana does. I reminded her about the notice and told her that on this occasion 'consideration of others' meant specifically consideration of me. "You didn't know I was so important, did you?"

When we were coming home after the show, I commented, "The hero's a new actor – he'll hardly get paid anything. Amitabh Bachchan will get the lion's share." To which she replied, "What, out of our seven pounds?"

User-friendly bathroom facilities

During his first week in England, a friend from Pakistan was greatly impressed by the bathroom facilities he encountered. At the end of this period of learning he observed: "When you sit on the toilet seat, it's so easy to relax! You can even rest your elbows on the cistern in front of you."

Moaning about the weather

When I first started my university course, I wanted to be very sociable, as I had been when in Pakistan. But I knew that English social etiquette would be different.

One such difference that I noticed immediately was the curious English expression 'Good Morning', used by everyone, for which there is no commonly-used equivalent in Urdu or Punjabi. I felt sure that this exotic greeting would be the key to my entry into student social life, and I began using it without reserve.

I wanted to copy the pronunciation exactly as delivered by the natives. So I was careful not to roll the 'r' of 'Good Morning', as an Asian person would be inclined to. But in my attempt, I seemed to miss out the letter altogether. Instead what I said sounded more like 'Good Moaning'.

Once when I said 'Good Moaning', another student turned round and pointed out of the window. "Look at the miserable weather," she commented. "Is that what you call a 'good' morning?"

I recalled instantly how people often said only 'Morning', rather than the complete '*Good* Morning', and now I knew why. The English language was even more rational than I had previously understood; even its greetings had descriptive power. There might have been any number of occasions when I'd used the phrase incorrectly, and exposed myself to ridicule!

I became very wary after that episode, and lost my enthusiasm. Before entering a classroom, I would look out at the weather. If it was sunny, I'd go in with a happy face and say 'Good Moaning'; and if it was overcast, with a glum face, just, 'Moaning'.

But even this led to more confusion. On occasion I would say 'Good Moaning', and receive the reply 'Morning', an apparently hostile denial of my opinion of the weather! I found it difficult to concentrate in class after such unpleasant conflicts.

Public spirit

When I was in Pakistan, people were usually frightened of the police, and tried to avoid them. Certainly it was unusual for anyone to volunteer to help them.

After coming to England, I started going to the local library and reading the newspapers. When reading crime reports, I was very impressed at how public-spirited so many people in this remarkable country were, in helping the police! A friend, who was rather cynical, wouldn't believe me, and he demanded to see proof for himself. I picked up a paper I had been reading earlier.

"Here you are, what do you make of this?"

And he read:

> **In the case of the murder of a prostitute in the Headingly area of Leeds, a resident of Bradford, Peter Sutcliffe, is helping the police with their enquiries.**

"What better proof could you want than this!" I said.

The life and soul of the party

Despite trying hard to socialise at university, I rarely ever attended any parties or other events. Sometimes, before the lecturer got to the classroom, a student would write a strange phrase on the blackboard – 'Disco Tonight!' – and although the significance of the announcement was beyond me, I knew for sure it wasn't anything to do with mathematics.

On one occasion, my tutor invited us to an evening party at his house in Leeds. I went along by bus, feeling very excited, eager to tell everyone my stories and jokes from Pakistan, and sure that this would make me the life and soul of the party. I was the first one to arrive.

But once the party got underway, I found myself abandoned in a corner of the room while the ten or so other guests mingled. Despite having travelled around the room, I was unable to edge my way into their conversations. The more time that passed, the more difficult it was to become involved, as if I might startle everyone with my presence! In the end, my only contribution to the party was to eat whatever was on offer.

In all the excitement of attending the party, I had not considered how I might return to Bradford after midnight. So when the party was finally over, it was my tutor himself who had to shoulder the burden of giving me a lift home. I was the last one to leave.

It was a winter's evening, and he couldn't have been very happy when he put on his overcoat, asked for my address, and we got into his car. I was feeling depressed and very embarrassed that while I had made no contribution to his party, I had nonetheless eaten his food and was now dragging him out in the middle of a cold night!

On our way, when we had still not exchanged a single word, I was feeling an urgent need to say something interesting to redeem myself. I spent minute after minute searching my mind for the most relevant thing to say. After spending some more time polishing up the question I was framing, I finally came out with:

"Sir, what is the difference, if any, between English mathematics and Russian mathematics?"

But he immediately interrupted, "Shush! I'm driving!"

So I had made two terrible blunders that evening. First, I had remained silent when required to speak, then I had spoken when required to remain silent. When he finally dropped me off at my house, I made sure not to commit a third blunder by saying '*good*night'.

"Night," I said.

"Goodnight," he replied.

A moving scene from Titanic

We once had a relative staying with us as a guest for a few days, a young man called Rashid. One evening he suggested that we might watch the video *Titanic* together. We had all seen the film before, though not together, and we had all enjoyed it very much. So we agreed to his suggestion.

The film contains a scene of female nudity, which Rashid must have forgotten about, for when this scene was reached Rashid directed his gaze towards his feet and said, "Rukhsana, quick! Fast-forward!" My wife was so panicked because of his unexpected sensibilities that she fumbled the remote-control, and by pressing the wrong button slowed the film down. She quickly tried again, but accidentally froze the picture in the critical pose! When Rashid lifted his gaze moments later, he had to rush out of the room.

Rukhsana finished her adjustment of the film, but Rashid didn't come back for a long time. We waited with the film paused at the next acceptable scene, but eventually decided to turn it off altogether.

When Rashid returned, no one mentioned the film. In fact no one mentioned films at all for the remainder of his visit.

Communicating with natives

Before coming to England, I would always pronounce the word 'alternative' as 'alter-*native*'. One of my friends would always try to correct me. "It's not 'alter-*native*'," he would say, "it's al-*ter*-native." I would get irritated, and rationalise my mistake by saying, "I can read it; I can write it correctly; I also know what it means. So what difference does it make how I pronounce it?" He eventually conceded the argument.

I lost contact with my friend, and it was after some 35 years that I again spoke to him, this time on the telephone from England. I reminded him of our old argument:

"Although you couldn't give any reasons at the time, you were right after all about the correct pronunciation of the word 'alternative'," I told him.

He was intrigued and wanted to find out what was so good about the 'correct' pronunciation. After all, I had given such a convincing argument for its unimportance.

"It's very simple," I said, finally admitting my mistake. "*The English didn't understand me* when I said 'alter-*native*'!"

Swimming lessons

Shortly after coming to England, I developed a desire to become a swimming instructor for Bradford Council, even though I was both unable to swim and afraid of water. To do this, I knew I would have to complete a swimming course first. Understanding my apprehension, one of my friends assured me that if I copied my instructor exactly, and followed instructions accurately, I should have no difficulty. Therefore, I enrolled in a swimming course at Shipley Swimming Pool.

Contrary to my expectations, I found that our instructress taught us without ever entering the pool. She gave us our first lesson while we were in the shallow end, and she was standing on the edge. She moved both of her arms and her left leg to demonstrate the arm and leg movements required. So I initially practised using both arms and only the left leg, following her demonstration precisely, as my friend had advised. Disappointingly, I was the only student who failed to make any progress during the first lesson.

If truth be told, I did not take easily to water. Breathing was my real problem. The method I adopted was to fill my lungs, then lunge forward as far as I could. But I always found that my head made straight for the bottom, and I would soon run out of breath. I would then stand up and repeat the process.

During every lesson, the instructress would say to me: "Unless you learn to come up for breath, you will kill yourself when you get to the deep end." I would always tell her: "My problem is how to keep my head above the water in the first place!" By the end of the introductory course, I had come to believe that the best solution to the breathing problem would be simply to stay out of the water altogether, and I decided to give up swimming.

But I didn't see why this should put me off my main aim of *teaching* swimming. After all, our instructress had gone through the whole course without once entering the water, and yet all her students, apart from me, had learned to swim well enough to go on to the next stage. I could remember all that the instructress had said to us, and could surely pass this on to others. With additional practice at home, I had perfected all her demonstrations. It need not be fatal to my application that I had failed the introductory course, because, as far as I could see, being able to swim was not actually relevant to teaching it. For all I knew, even the instructress herself may have been unable to swim!

My friend, who knew about these things, told me that the Council would not be able to appreciate this reasoning, and in the end I decided not to apply for the job. However, my friend assured me there was no need to feel sad: the experience had revealed that being a swimming instructor – once alluringly challenging – was in fact far too simple for a man of my potential.

The Queen's English vs. Asian English

Ideas come first, and words are subservient to the ideas. However, the way English is used in the Indian subcontinent doesn't always reflect this fact. For instance, being an Asian speaker of English, and having built up a repertoire of more difficult English words (although I'm still unclear about the meaning of some!), I tend to look for appropriate occasions to use them.

In the Indian subcontinent, difficult, obscure and less well-understood words are often taken to reflect education and scholarship. To sprinkle our Urdu or Hindi conversation with English words suggests that we have been to England or America, and, therefore, gives status and prestige. This way of enhancing status is quite common in the conversations of the heroes and heroines in Indian films, where they sometimes speak whole English sentences, followed by their Hindi translations. This is to achieve two objectives – first to impress, and then to enlighten.

Furthermore, speaking quickly in English is highly respected. This is so even if the English happens to be full of errors. People are reluctant to ask for clarification, for fear of accidentally exposing their own poor grasp of the language.

When people speak good English with reflective pauses, they are often interpreted as having difficulty finding their words. Indeed, when taken at speed, an Asian person's English is often more awe-inspiring than the natural flow of an English native.

All of this leads to an unfortunate result, in that the speaker who is considered by common folk to be the most educated, impressive and profound, is in fact the least understood!

Use of definite article 'the'

Word in English language, usage of which is most difficult to master by Asians, is definite article. Reason for our difficulty is that we do not have even concept represented by this word, let alone equivalent word, in Urdu or Hindi. Way this word is sprinkled in an English text is quite mysterious for an Asian. But Asian languages neither lack precision nor suffer any other loss by absence of abominable creature.

Real question is: what is it about English language that would make it almost stifle without oxygen of definite article, whereas Asian languages breathe quite freely? Is there something inherent in English language that makes definite article so essential to it?

Trillions of hours of work have been given over to study of this word by Asian learner of English. Many chapters and many books have been written on subject, and they generally fail to completely explain its use. Even most learned Asians can never completely escape feeling of unease that accompanies their attempts to put what they have learned into practice.

Those Asian learners of English who go on to become translators can achieve at least a little recompense for all their troubles. For example, at rate of 25p per word, a translation into Urdu of an English text involving 100 occurrences of definite article will earn translator an extra £25 for doing nothing at all – just about enough to buy yet another book on subject.

A student's respect

In Pakistan, when asking a question in class, it was obligatory to raise your hand and stand up. It was considered to be respectful of the teacher.

At Leeds University, I found it difficult to show my teachers the same respect. This was because all the desks overhung the seats, making it impossible to fully rise. Whenever I had a question, I would partially rise and be seen to cower at the teacher.

Portrait of a bus conductor

When I was a student at Leeds University in 1971, I wanted to make some extra money at the weekends. So I put a notice in a local Asian butcher's, advertising my skills as a Mathematics tutor. As a result of this, I started teaching the children of a Mohammed Din, who had been in England since the 1950s. He was a bus conductor in Bradford, and he eventually became a good friend.

He told me that when he had been in Pakistan he had been a *Patwari*. A Patwari is a revenue official whose duties involve land measurements to be included in registry records. Although the profession is ranked lowly by officials, it gives a man status in the eyes of others, particularly those who own land. Din much valued the status he had acquired through his work.

However, upon coming to England and obtaining a job as a trainee worker in a mill, he was highly distressed when at the end of the shift he was told that his duties required him to sweep his work area clean. One of his fellow workers told him not to worry: that he would soon get used to it, just as everyone else had. But Din didn't want to get used to it. For him, a broom was a sign of low standing, and he wept at the thought of a lifetime of using one.

As it turned out, he didn't stay at the mill very long, but soon had a job as a bus conductor, working for the local authority in Bradford. The job of bus conductor didn't have the status of Patwari, but it satisfied him well enough, and he stayed with it for the rest of his working life. However, all his friends, including me, continued to call him 'Patwari Saab' or 'Patwari ji', titles which express the esteem in which he was held. Din himself would always extend me the same degree of respect by calling me 'Master Saab', on account of my experience as a teacher in Pakistan.

Din was a simple man from Mirpur, Pakistan, and his way of life was characterised by Eastern hospitality. Though not himself well educated, he was a great believer in the value of education. Not only would he pay me the tuition fees for his children, but when the lessons were over, he would never let me leave his house without first offering me some curry and chapattis.

Some would have called Din cute, for he was a short, plump man, with a nose like a koala's and a plodding side-to-side gait to match. But he wore a long twirling moustache that gave him an impressive, even formidable, appearance, and he would always recommend that I grow a similar one.

His uniform consisted of a heavy, thick, dark green overcoat, with jacket and black trousers, together with a peaked hat. For a number of reasons, he would wear his uniform in all seasons, even when he was off duty. Firstly, he did not want to go through the hassle of having to prove that he qualified for free rides on Bradford buses – his uniform was proof enough. Secondly, when the 'government' (as he would put it) had given him a warm uniform and a hat, why should he spend money on his own clothing?

"But why do you wear such a warm uniform even in summer?" I once queried, being very frank.

"They are very good at absorbing sweat!" he adroitly justified himself.

But his reasons did not dilute the mystery of his wearing the uniform all the time. Most of the bus drivers and bus conductors knew him well and would certainly have allowed him to travel free without him wearing his uniform.

This mystery was eventually resolved when I once paid him a surprise visit late in the evening and saw him without his hat on. When he saw me through the door, he panicked and immediately grabbed a nearby tea towel and wrapped it around his head. But it was too late. His secret had been revealed. I had seen quite clearly that he was bald.

Only on festive occasions such as Eid would he wear his own traditional Eastern attire. But this included a black *Jinnah* cap which continued to protect his baldness from prying eyes. At these times, without his uniform, it became easier to see most of him as he really was, though it would be difficult to recognise him on the street with such reduced dimensions.

On one festive occasion, I saw him wearing unusually colourful socks – one red and one yellow.

"That's a rare pair of socks you have on today, Patwari Saab," I said in jest. "Who are you trying to impress?"

"Oh, they're not really so very rare at all," he said. "I've got another pair just like them at home!"

Din's humour was illustrated on another occasion, when I asked him for the date. He didn't know, and I suggested that he consult the newspaper he had sticking out of his pocket.

"Oh, that's no good," he said. "It's yesterday's paper!"

When we were out together I had to remain alert when we crossed roads. When Din started to cross, he would concentrate hard on what he was doing, his speed would decrease, and he would drop behind me. But when he reached the middle of the road, his policy changed. He would suddenly sprint past me, head down and hands in his pockets, leaving me to cross the remainder of the road alone. His explanation was that after reaching the mid-point, it was too late to make a U-turn and dash back to the start. Once fully committed to making the crossing, he went as fast as possible.

When I was out with him I would be impressed by the fact that so many English people knew him well. And he would always lift his hand, and greet them, regardless of their age, uttering his standard phrase: "Good morning, boss!"

If I bumped into Din in town, he would always take me to a nearby restaurant, and buy me a scone and a cup of tea. On some of these occasions, while I was drinking he would take out an official form, turned into a wad by excessive folding, which he would have kept for me to fill in for him. With a cup of tea and a scone in front of me, I was even more happy to help. Even though his children were doing O Levels and A Levels, he always treated them as not experienced enough in worldly matters, and he had such trust in my academic abilities that he would always request me, rather than his children, to write his letters, or fill in his forms.

When we left the restaurant he would then travel with me and pay for my bus fare. Or, if he knew the bus conductor, which would often be the case, I would travel as Din's guest without a ticket.

When at work and giving tickets, Din would often round the fares down, letting passengers off the odd penny or two. He would find it embarrassing to insist on such trivial amounts. On the other hand, he would have found it equally embarrassing to insist on giving back a penny or two in change to anyone, and he would never do so. In the course of a day's duty he would break about even, as well as maintaining the Eastern tradition of avoiding penny-pinching. He told me that he was once reprimanded by an inspector who did a spot check, and watched him walk away from a passenger who still had his hand extended for a penny change! Din had taken this reprimand in his stride, and had continued with his traditional service. He enjoyed great respect among his colleagues.

If I travelled on a bus on which he was working, he would generally not come to me with a ticket, but he sometimes felt obliged to give me one for reasons only known to him. Perhaps he'd anticipated a spot check by one of the inspectors. On these occasions, although he gave me a ticket, he would push my hand away when I held out my fare. This meant that he would have to pay my fare himself, either straightaway, or when he reached the garage. On one such occasion I happened to look at the ticket just after getting off the bus – it read £0.01!

Din was a paragon of truth, simplicity, and honesty – a magnanimous creature from another world. On one occasion he went into an office and, after his usual greeting of "Good morning, boss!" he asked the manager whether there was a job for his son.

"I'm afraid there's no vacancy at the moment," the manager said apologetically.

"No need to be afraid!" he replied. "If there is no vacancy at the moment, I can come back in the afternoon." As he left, his face was beaming with great expectation.

Din once complained to me about an unemployed friend of his called Karim. "When I get home at eleven o' clock, after working ten hours, I find Karim waiting for a chat at my house. I can't stay up for long, as I have to get up early in the morning. But Karim never wants to go. I don't know how to ask him to leave. What should I do?"

"Tell him you won't be able to wake up the following morning," I sympathetically advised him.

"Yes, I did tell him exactly that," said Din. "But Karim said, 'No need to worry. I'll come round and wake you up!' So I couldn't refuse him."

Sadly there are no more bus conductors in Bradford. Din lost the use of his uniform when he retired, and I haven't seen him since. I have it from reliable sources that he has returned to the Himalayas, where he must be enjoying his British pension.

A breathtaking honeymoon

The 'honeymoon' is a well-established concept in the West, but a relatively new one in the Indian subcontinent, not at all well understood among older village folk at the time of my marriage to my wife Rukhsana. No wonder we haven't got an exact translation for the word 'honeymoon', and that the English word itself has to be used by Urdu or Hindi speakers. On the other hand, we have the words *Suhaag Raat* (for the first night of a marriage), for which there is no English equivalent.

Shortly after our marriage, Rukhsana and I decided to be modern, and to have a short and slightly belated honeymoon in Murree, a resort in the foothills of the Himalayas. When my parents and my father-in-law (who was visiting) discovered our plans, they insisted that, as they hadn't seen Murree before, they would also like to go on the honeymoon with us – without, of course, knowing what this word meant! We could not explain it to them, as our upbringing didn't allow us to be very frank with our parents, particularly in such matters. So we reluctantly conceded to their desire, and took them along with us. As we would have to meet all the costs, the honeymoon would now have to be reduced to just two nights.

We caught a minibus bound for Murree from a nearby town, Saddar Bazaar. My parents sat together and my father-in-law sat separately with another passenger. When they were all settled down on their seats, they immediately started chatting with the passengers sitting nearby, as old people do.

"Where are you going *Baba ji*?" one passenger asked my father.

"We are going on honeymoon!" my father replied, with great pride and excitement.

"What about you, Baba ji?" someone asked my father-in-law.

"I am going on honeymoon as well," he said, pointing to my father, "with him."

When we got to Murree, we had to look for accommodation straightaway, in case we should experience difficulty finding any in the evening. Very soon we were beckoned over by a man who recognised us as tourists, and he said he could show us some good places to stay. We followed him down a winding path through pine trees, to where there were two apartments: one of them had only one room and the other had two.

The man, who was acting for the owner, explained the rates. After listening to him, my father said thoughtfully, "If we all squeeze into the one room, we'll be able to stay twice as long. We can manage with less space, can't we?" So we paid for four nights' accommodation in a single room for all of us – Rukhsana and myself, both my parents and my father-in-law: five people, three single beds. No one objected to my father-in-law having one of these for himself, though it was a tight squeeze for the rest of us.

During the night, my father, who suffered from asthma, had an attack. In the morning we decided, to our great disappointment, that as the cold climate in Murree was aggravating Father's condition, we would have to return home straightaway. So we came back that evening, even though we had paid for four nights. Without my father's innovative approach to the room booking, we could have had two rooms that night, for the same money!

On our way back, my father-in-law told the passengers sitting next to him, "I had a wonderful honeymoon, even though we had to cut our stay short." Whereas my father said with some disappointment, "We came here on honeymoon as well, but I got short of breath on the first night, so we're having to go back home early."

The subdivided Indian subcontinent

I very much doubt whether there are any other bordering countries in the world which have such a wealth of common heritage, common culture, and natural affinity as India and Pakistan. In fact, they had been *one country* for centuries, and, but for the British Raj and the subsequent granting of independence, perhaps we would have remained as one.

Religious differences caused Partition, and yet the Muslim population of both countries is now about the same. I daresay that, in the three wars the two countries have fought since winning independence from Britain in 1947, Muslim soldiers from each of the two sides have found themselves dropping bombs on Muslim soldiers of the other. How could the people of *one country, who lived together as neighbours for centuries*, suddenly become each other's deadly enemies just because a handful of people drew a political border between them?

As a result of Partition, lots of people born in India now live in Pakistan, and vice versa. They have difficulty in seeing their places of birth just across the border, or their relatives who stayed behind at Partition. A stunning example is that the Heads of State of India and Pakistan in 2008 had been born in each other's country. That is, an Indian Muslim was Head of the Islamic Republic of Pakistan, and a Pakistani Sikh was Head of the Republic of India!

As time goes on, and because of Partition, the Pakistani Muslims are becoming much more alienated and distanced from the Hindus across the border than the Indian Muslims are from the same Hindu neighbours. We should try to reverse this unfortunate trend towards alienation, if possible.

India and Pakistan own a myriad of the world's most beautiful areas, with cultures and religions as diverse as the people. We have the most beautiful valleys, which nestle in the folds of the highest mountains in the world, the Himalayas. Here we find Kashmir, Ladakh, Himachal Pradesh, Sikkim and Darjeeling, before which the beauty of any European landscape pales into insignificance. Such stunningly beautiful places should belong to the whole of the subcontinent across which they stretch – some 2,000 miles. The natural partition of the mountains does not correspond with the man-made political partitioning we have imposed. When there is an earthquake, it is as though the mountains themselves are crying out to tell us how foolish we are!

How marvellous it would be if we, India and Pakistan, could put Europe to shame with our unity, our science and our technology. The colossal sums of money that we spend to buy armaments from the West, so as to be able to kill each other, help run *their* welfare states. Why not divert these funds to enhance the welfare of our own people? The world would then look upon us with envy! Instead of US dollars and British pounds dominating the global markets, I imagine our Rupee leading while other currencies follow. Our economy could be vastly stronger, and instead of one pound being equal to a hundred rupees, it could be the other way round!

I also wish we had immigration problems like the West. I have a vision of people from Europe and America aspiring to come to us, legally or illegally, in spite of soaring unemployment on the subcontinent (some on a pretext of seeking asylum) and applying for *our* nationality. We would then hold some of them in our Immigration Removal Centres, and deport them on the grounds that their presence was *'not conducive to the public good'*, and give those who had been given *'indefinite leave to remain'* an Urdu test, and another test in Asian cultures, religions and colonial history, in order to see whether they qualify to become good citizens of the Indian subcontinent. After every 15 or 20 years we would announce a General Amnesty for all those foreigners who had managed to escape the tentacles of our Home Office, so that they need no longer allow themselves to be exploited for pittance wages.

This is my vision of the Indian subcontinent, which, I am proud to say, is my ancestral home.

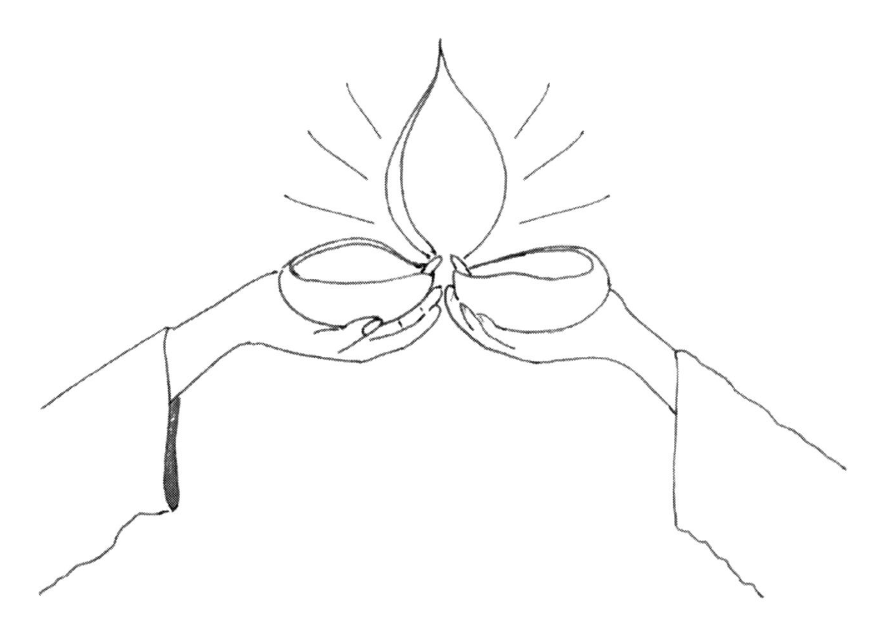

India and Pakistan

England as Seen by Chacha

England as Seen by Chacha

My father, Punnu Khan, then 68, and my mother, Noor Begum, then 63, left their remote village in Pakistan in 1978, and came to join us in England. My father, whom we would call 'Chacha' (which really means 'Uncle'), was very impressed by a number of things here, particularly by the marvels of science and technology. But he could never quite make up his mind. His strict Muslim views about morality and his perception of the world were very traditional, and this led to his being very disturbed by some of the things he met here in England.

Gateway to England

On his first arrival at Bradford train station, Chacha made his way with me to the exit. He'd almost touched the double doors in order to push them open, when they suddenly flung themselves outwards, panicking him considerably. I walked through, and as he followed me he asked for an explanation. I told him that these English doors can 'see' when they need to open.

Not believing any of this, Chacha immediately turned around and tried the doors once again for himself. Sure enough, the doors opened automatically. But still feeling sceptical, he made a few more dives in and out, to give my claim a thorough testing. All the while, he was totally oblivious to those around him, some of whom were regarding him with great interest.

At last, Chacha looked at me, nodded his head approvingly, and said: "My boy, you're absolutely right. English science is really impressive. No one could catch these doors off-guard!"

Chacha on the British transport system

Chacha was quite used to the muddy and dusty roads of Pakistan where *tongas* and rickshaws were a common sight. Compared to this, the transport system throughout Britain was a technological marvel. Consider how it is that such dense traffic is safely controlled on roundabouts, junctions, flyovers and motorways.

Chacha was aware that dense traffic led to harmful pollution. So when he saw the roads in England, he said: "Look what all these cars and lorries do! There's so much exhaust, the roads have even turned black!"

Despite this, Chacha was highly impressed by what he observed. He commented one day on how advanced the modern vehicles were. "British cars have amazing mirrors," he said. "They reverse images of all words except 'Ambulance'." On a another occasion, Chacha praised the ingenious technology which allowed the cat's eyes on main roads to be activated only when it became dark, and only when needed by approaching vehicles.

False sense of security

Chacha thought it strange that all the houses in England have glass windows, that some have glass doors, and that some houses even have glass walls; and yet that the doors of these houses might be secured by 5-lever locks! Chacha perceived an incongruity between the strength of the locks and the apparent fragility of the rest of the house.

Cultural divide

Britain is a country of diverse people. Given any subject, you'll find people whose views are at opposite extremes.

It is not uncommon to see two ladies sitting on a bench, one at each end, one Asian and the other English. The first can be covered from head to foot in a black veil, while the other by comparison is almost naked! The uncovered area of English woman at one end of the bench would be much the same as the total covered area of Muslim at the other. Chacha was tired when he came across such a scene one day, but he decided not to sit down in the middle.

The trolley trade

I used to take Chacha with me to one of the local supermarkets. Here you can obtain a trolley by pushing a £1 coin into it, to release it from the other trolleys in the stack. You can later on recover your coin when it is released from the trolley as you return it.

One day, I saw a man taking his trolley back to park it. To save time I offered him my £1 coin for his trolley, a common practice among shoppers. Chacha was watching me with interest. He nodded his head. "These English trolleys are incredibly cheap," Chacha said with astonishment.

Free cash withdrawals

Chacha was astounded by the use of credit cards for shopping. Once, after we had left the supermarket with our groceries, he commented, "At home, when you go to the shops they give you goods, but you have to give them money in exchange. Here, when they give you the goods it doesn't cost you anything. You just give them that little piece of plastic. Then they give it back to you, and they even offer to give you some cash back as well. What a country!"

Water conservation

I was interested to discover how Chacha handled the water taps in some public toilets. I once came across him pushing again and again on a hand basin tap, one of those designed to turn themselves off after a few seconds.

"What are you doing, Chacha?" I asked.

"I'm trying to turn the tap off," he said, "but it just keeps on coming and coming. What a waste!"

A selective sweet tooth

Chacha found it odd that most English people are willing to accept chocolates, biscuits or cakes, but when they are offered tea, they most often say, "No sugar, thank you!" Hardly anyone in Pakistan takes tea without sugar.

A hat trick

Chacha was favourably impressed by the practice of queuing he encountered in England. In Pakistan, a bus-stop attracts not a queue but a crowd. When the bus arrives, mayhem reigns as people race to get on as quickly as possible. Chacha was a slight, mild-mannered man, and didn't like to enter into this rough and tumble.

But Chacha was resourceful and, understanding something of crowd psychology, was often able to secure a place on Pakistani buses. What he did was to sneak around the bus and put his *topi* through an open window onto a seat, to give the impression that a friend had saved a place for him or that someone had left the bus temporarily. He was then able to stand behind the crowd and board at leisure after everyone else. His place would always have been left vacant for him.

His explanation of this was that the first passengers on the bus had no reason to occupy 'his' place, and so they sat elsewhere. The ones who sat around his topi would then guard his place for him against other passengers, some of whom would have to stand. When Chacha eventually arrived he would pick up his topi, put it on his head, and settle down in his 'reserved' seat, thanking nearby passengers for keeping it safe for him.

Chacha's topi

Only on one occasion was Chacha's plan foiled. Chacha boarded the bus to find that his 'reserved' place was now occupied by a very self-assured looking giant of a man, on whose head Chacha's topi was now resting. Chacha decided not to pursue any claim – either for the seat, or for the topi – and stood innocently for the remainder of the journey, as if nothing had happened.

When Chacha arrived in England he was happy to find that there were none of the difficulties that applied to buses in Pakistan, and that he was able to obtain a seat by the simple expedient of arriving in good time and standing in line. This was fortunate, as the windows were generally all closed.

Spitting: a disgusting habit?

There was a young man from Darjeeling
Who boarded a bus bound for Ealing.
He saw on the door
'Please don't spit on the floor',
So he stood up and spat on the ceiling.

Anonymous

Among the things I told Chacha about English customs was that English people don't spit. "It's thought to be disgusting," I said.

"What do they do instead?" Chacha asked in puzzlement.

"They use a hanky, or swallow it down."

"Ugh! Ugh!! Ugh!!! That's even worse!" Chacha recoiled.

Wink, wink

Winking generally has a much stronger sexual connotation for Asians than for the English. Chacha knew nothing of the friendly conspiratorial wink, and his first contact with it was highly disconcerting for him.

Canine conundrum

Chacha was never able to share the English liking for dogs. He could not understand why their owners would supply them with jackets, would take them out for exercise, and especially why they would clean up after them in the park. He was astounded when he learned that dogs in England even receive medical attention. He said that in England the dogs receive better care than poor people do in Pakistan.

He was even more intrigued to notice that English people actually speak to their dogs, and on top of this, the dogs seemed to understand what was being said.

Chacha had seen a sign at the entrance to our local park which showed a picture of a dog, and which greatly mystified him. One day, when we were out walking, he asked me about it. I said that the sign announced that the area was a 'Clean-It-Up Dog Zone' and that non-compliance would result in a maximum fine of £1,000.

"So you see," I explained, "the reason why the English clean up after their dogs is not just to avoid a public nuisance, it's also to avoid a hefty fine."

"Well I'm glad to hear that the *dogs* aren't meant to read the notice and pay the fines," Chacha observed.

The logic of English hygiene

Chacha had a highly developed concern for hygiene. He found it strange that in a country where his concern was shared in most respects, people would nevertheless wipe their dirty shoes on the door mat. As he saw it, any sort of dirt might be wiped off onto the mat; this dirt would then be transferred to the mail and the newspapers, and from there to the breakfast table. "Ugh," said Chacha.

The English of the English

Almost everyone in Pakistan knows that the Urdu word *'kitaab'* means 'book' in English. In fact, the two words are interchangeable in the spoken language of Pakistan.

We were in the library one day, when Chacha bewailed the fact that his poor English made it difficult to communicate. But I was able to make him feel better. I told him that he knew some English words that even English people might not know. To illustrate this for him I turned to the librarian at the desk.

"Do you happen to know the English word for *'kitaab'*?" I asked.

As I had anticipated, the librarian shook his head and said he didn't know the word. Chacha was amazed and really quite pleased that an English person could be ignorant of such a simple English word as 'book', a word he himself had known since childhood – especially as this particular Englishman worked in a library.

Ants in their pants

"They are like ants!" Chacha used to say of the English. I once asked him what he meant.

"Take any solitary Englishman," he said. "He is relaxed, not doing much, just walking along slowly and aimlessly, as if on holiday.

"But what happens when he meets some others? Once they get together they turn into a well-organised and formidable workforce, with architects and foremen and masons and bricklayers. They run around producing motorways and factories and skyscrapers. Wherever they have settled, they have transformed the land, be it Canada, Australia or America. They can't help themselves, any more than ants can."

Up to no good

"The English are always searching for something," Chacha once said. "It might be in the depths of the sea, it might be on the top of Mount Everest. The other day, someone told me they have been to the Moon, and I know they have sent what they call 'probes' even further into Space. They can't be doing all this searching for nothing, these clever monkeys! I'm sure they must have a hidden agenda, but I just can't figure out what it is. No doubt we'll find out in the end!"

Getting a feel for Britain

Chacha said that there is always more to discover about Britain. "Finding out about Britain is rather like being blind from birth, and trying to discover what an elephant is like. You feel different parts of the elephant, and might even come to mistakenly believe that you know what it is like. But there will always be a lot that you have not yet come across, and you might be in for a big surprise."

Britain, as seen by Chacha

Artificial intelligence

"The British don't use their minds," Chacha said. "They use electricity and computers instead. When the electricity runs out, Britain will grind to a halt."

Antiques

Chacha was quite unable to understand the value given to antiques by the English. "They are prepared to bid thousands of pounds at an auction for worn-out old furniture, which I would chuck out on a tip. How can it be that people who are generally so intelligent will lose their minds when they have a chance to acquire old junk!"

Does a little help go a long way?

Asking directions in this country can have its pitfalls. When Chacha asked the way to the station, the English shopkeeper he asked was simply too obliging in his response. The exhaustive details he provided about the route left Chacha's head in a whirl, and this only led to more and more details being given. A simple 'Straight ahead, second right and there it is on the left' would have done. But in the end three or four shoppers became involved as well, making Chacha more and more confused.

He later told me that when he left the shop it was only by luck that he found his way to the station at all, and that in any case he had by then missed the train! Those who helped him had concentrated entirely on how to get to the station, and had forgotten the real purpose behind his request – that is, to catch his train!

The puzzle of Europe

Chacha became very serious one day. "In spite of alcohol, premarital sex, pornography, nudity and homosexuality, Europe is ahead of the world in science and technology, health, affluence and leadership. Europe should have been doomed, so how *can* it be so successful?" Chacha was in a quandary.

Making up

In Asian cultures, fair skin is held to be very beautiful. For this reason, it is common for Asian women to wear makeup that makes brown faces lighter. With this fact in mind, Chacha found it difficult to understand why English women, whose skin is already fair, would use makeup at all.

From chilli to chilly

Chacha had been used to a warm climate before he came to England. When winter came, Chacha was surprised how the English could cope with it. "Look at the English women," he said. "They walk around with bare legs, even in this weather. Are they immune to the cold?"

But Chacha said that what struck him most about the cold weather was that getting into bed at night was as difficult as getting out of bed in the morning.

Public nudity

Chacha was totally against public nudity. He believed in one's immutable duty to cover oneself up. He was surprised when he discovered that there are those in England who seek to demonstrate their right to go about as naked as the day they were born.

It is not difficult to know what his attitude would have been to one modern disciple of nudity, Stephen Gough, who some years ago walked naked from Land's End to John O'Groats to prove his point. Although there was controversy about his exploit, and he spent some time in prison, he nevertheless received much public support. Ultimately, the courts which considered the matter of his pilgrimage allowed it to continue (though the judge had insisted that the accused remain seated throughout the court proceedings).

When the news of Mr Gough's court victory was given on TV, I imagined Chacha turning in his grave. However, Nature celebrated Mr Gough's release with a quick burst of snow. I imagine this would have helped Chacha to rest again.

The reward of virtue

One day I gave Chacha my favourite quotation from Bertrand Russell: '*Remember your humanity and forget the rest*'.

"Too much of the world," I said, "seems to live by the maxim 'Forget your humanity and remember the rest'."

Chacha gave this a lot of thought. Eventually he said he was sorry for all the non-Muslims in the world.

"Poor things!" he said. "It doesn't really matter what they do. Even if they spend their lives doing good deeds, they'll all go to Hell in the end!"

A sad irony

When I told Chacha that I intended to one day write a book in English, in which he was to play an important role, he heaved a great sigh. He said that quite a lot of people who could most benefit from reading certain books, are, like him, unable to read or write.

Science and Philosophy

Science and Philosophy

God's spaceship

A long time ago, when I was in Pakistan, a friend of mine told me, "The Russian and American astronauts, wearing spacesuits, are going to meet in Space, on the other side of the Earth, over the Atlantic Ocean. What a success for space science!"

To put space science in its place, I retorted, "That's nothing compared with God's science! Using God's spaceship, even you and I can meet up in Space, wearing ordinary clothes. We could have a cup of tea on the other side of the Sun, a hundred and ninety million miles from here!"

He thought I was joking. But, no! We did meet in Space on the other side of the Sun, six months later, and had a cup of tea together.

The scale of the cosmos

Chacha had once learnt something about the stars. He would tell us, now and again, when we were young, that we mustn't think that the stars are as small as they appear to the naked eye.

"Not at all!" he would say, stretching his arms as wide as they would reach. "They're as big as *that*!"

Life in a ping-pong ball

Imagine you were born and bred in a ping-pong ball, and spent the whole of your life in there. Between matches, when you have time to reflect, can you ever acquire knowledge of what's going on in the outside world?

You have access to the best laboratories inside the ball and any equipment you need. The only input from the outside world is in the form of bumps and jolts during the matches. Even if you somehow learn that you inhabit a ping-pong ball, could you ever work out the rules of the game?

Perhaps our situation is not so very different from this.

A scientist's professional prestige

Suppose that a world famous scientist has established his fame and credibility on the basis of his successful research, which had led to accurate predictions. Now suppose that after a lifetime of research he makes a final prediction that, on such-and-such a date, Great Britain will be overcome by some specified natural disaster.

His professional prestige and fame now hinge on the accuracy of this prediction. As the time approaches, would he find it easy to hope that his prediction should turn out to be false?

Chacha's formidable challenge to world scientists

I once extolled the wonder of modern machines to Chacha, but on this occasion he was not impressed. He said we take Nature's own machines too much for granted. To illustrate this, he presented me with a challenge which I have set out below:

> *I hereby challenge you to make a machine – with 1 input and 2 outputs – which can convert grass into any of the following pairs of substances:*
>
> a) *Buffalo milk and buffalo dung*
> b) *Goat's milk and goat droppings*
>
> *Or for the more confident scientist:*
>
> c) *Buffalo milk and goat droppings*
> d) *Goat's milk and buffalo dung*

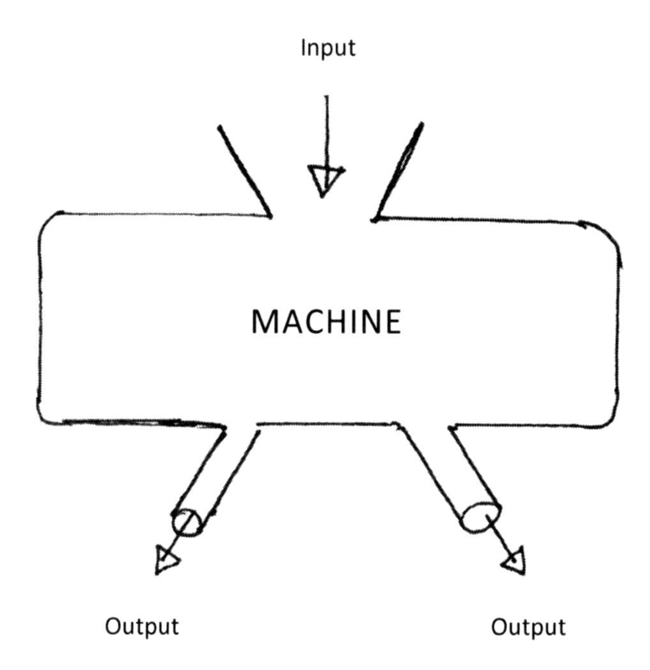

Craze for mobile phones

There was a time when, if we had found someone by himself talking to the air and holding his ear, we would have been inclined to cross over and walk on the other side of the road. Now we are in a predicament, as we find such people on both sides of the road.

Helpful answer-phones

So far, telephone technology cannot be relied upon to provide us with the phone numbers of those who call us from overseas.

One day, my new machine said to me in a helpful voice: "You have one new message." It was from my wife Rukhsana who was in Rawalpindi, Pakistan, at the time.

"Mahmud!" she called down the phone, aware of the poor reception. "Rukhsana speaking. I've just arrived; take a note of my number – I hope you can hear me! Listen carefully. It's 0-0, 9-2, 5-1, 9-3-6-4-6. That's 0-0, 9-2, 5-1, 9-3-6-4-6. I hope you heard that. I'll say it again: 0-0, 9-2, 5-1, 9-3-6-4-6. That's 0-0, 9-2, 5-1, 9-3-6-4-6."

After the message, the helpful voice returned: "You were called today at eight thirty-six. We do not have the caller's number to return the call."

Philosophy on the brain

Whatever philosophy is, it isn't science. Since philosophy doesn't require our senses, I don't believe it can tell us anything about the physical world.

With pure thought alone, we cannot even know the shape or size of our brain, despite it being the very seat of the same thoughts. Nor could we know where it is in our body, or even whether it exists anywhere at all!

Taming the bicycle

Riding a bike is based upon sound scientific principles. But just sitting up on one and peddling is not going to get you anywhere, even if you know the science. A special sense of balance is needed, possessed by only man and monkeys and a few other forms of life. Will a robot ever be built that can ride my bike?

The design of the bicycle is not just based on sound scientific principles to do with gravity – it also requires some principles *to do with us*. But if you look at a human being and a bike dispassionately, it is not at all obvious that the one will be able to ride the other. If the inventor of the bicycle actually foresaw that this man-made, two-legged, metallic animal could be tamed, with perseverance on the part of the trainer, then I salute him, and his science!

The probability of forgetfulness

Suppose a friend of mine has arranged to come to see me every Sunday at 4pm, but that half the times he forgets and does not turn up. Suppose also that, on one occasion, I ask him to cancel the following Sunday's get-together. What are the odds of his turning up this time?

An astronomical insight

"If people hadn't had any eyes, there wouldn't have been any astronomy," I put to Chacha one day, "and we wouldn't have known there were any planets or stars."

He gave this some thought. "I see. If we'd all been blind," he said, "we wouldn't have been able to make telescopes."

The power of our atmosphere

Suppose you go to the Lake District in the north of England. At Lake Windermere you are held up in a colossal traffic jam caused by the coming and going of hundreds of container-lorries. On enquiring, you are told that water from the lake is being taken away to Switzerland, as part of Britain's contribution towards refilling Lake Geneva – the largest lake in Europe – which has mysteriously been found empty.

Surely, you think, the refilling of Lake Geneva must be the greatest transport exercise of all time! Indeed, you think, it hardly seems possible.

Here is an even more impossible exercise: suppose that you woke up one day to find that all the lakes and non-tidal rivers of the world were empty and all the mountains denuded of ice and snow. There would be only one place to obtain the water required to restore their former glory: the sea. But not even the entire human resources of the world would be sufficient to transport enough water from the sea to replace what had disappeared.

Despite the apparently insurmountable difficulties, this is precisely the problem which is being solved all the time in the world, right now, by Nature. How otherwise would the missing water have got to where it had been in the first place?

Water is being taken all the time from the sea and transported across the world, to be deposited in the rivers and lakes as rain, and on the mountains as snow. It is taken by air, that is to say, by our atmosphere.

Our atmosphere achieves this by liaising with the Sun. The Sun causes sea water to evaporate, leading to a pressure difference between the atmosphere and the vapour. The atmosphere presses down on the vapour which then rises up to where the pressure is less.

In this way the atmosphere is at work all day long, loading the sea into clouds, ready for transportation. Air transport around the world is again achieved by differences in pressure.

This time, the differences are between one part of the atmosphere and others, caused by the heat of the Sun.

This gigantic task is performed every day and all day long, has been going on for aeons, and is generally unappreciated by those who benefit.

Gaining weight

I once asked Chacha how we gain weight.

"Simple!" he said. "We gain weight when more goes in than comes out! Didn't you study science?"

Quadrilateral thinking

The neatest and most elegant way to find the centre of a square is to find the point of intersection of the two diagonals.

What is the most *cumbersome* way of finding the centre that you can think of?

Ignorance has its own power

An ignorant person cannot fully understand a knowledgeable person. But nor can a knowledgeable person fully understand an ignorant person. The knowledgeable person's ignorance can be much more serious than the ignorant person's.

Newton and the snake

I had just been telling my friend Din that Isaac Newton's Laws of Motion explain how our legs propel us along.

"Well," Din said, "what about snakes? How can a snake move forward without legs – when it's never even heard of Newton?"

If I were a bird...

If I were a bird, I would not sit serenely, pecking and un-ruffling my feathers, on the high-power lines between pylons, oblivious to the danger-signs of barbed wire and the painted notice depicting skull and cross-bones down below – even if I knew all the physics.

The very thought of sitting on these live wires with thousands of volts of electricity passing through them is horrendous. Brave birds!

A brave bird

God left out of the equation

Chacha would always get puzzled about those world-famous scientists and philosophers who don't believe in God. He would say: "Even an ignorant person like myself, who doesn't know any philosophy or science and can't even sign his own name, knows that God exists. I can't understand why such educated people have difficulty – especially given the advantages of believing in God and the disadvantages of not believing. Haven't they ever heard of Hell?"

Perpetual motion machine

> *"If I could climb the first step of a staircase, I could climb them all!"*
>
> *Mahmud Khan, The Logic of Half a Moustache, 2010*

Suppose I am trying to produce a perpetual motion machine, that is, a moving system which never stops if left alone.

So I drop a bouncy ball in my study every now and again. Although it does not quite reach the same height on bouncing back, I know that if it *just once* reached the same height, I'd have succeeded in producing such a machine. There would be no reason for it not to return to the same height again, and again, and again. That is logic!

So I keep trying from different heights and in different places. You never know, one day I might succeed in producing a simple perpetual motion machine. Am I being logical?

A timely getaway

Imagine there are sixty-one people in a queue at a bank, and that the queue reduces at the rate of one person per minute. Suppose I go into the bank and notice that a friend of mine is at the head of the queue. We briefly exchange greetings, then, just as he goes to the counter, I take his place at the head of the queue rather than join it at the back. Every one of the other sixty people in the queue would lose one minute each, and I would gain *one hour*!

How does it come about that, although my gain of one hour is immediate, the corresponding loss of one minute each for the other customers is deferred for anything up to one hour? In fact, by the time the last person in the queue has lost his minute, I will have had a full hour in which to make my getaway!

Light entertainment

Chacha was very proud that I was learning science when I was at college, and he would sometimes challenge me.

"My son," he said one day, "if you had two parallel mirrors, could you make a beam of light go backwards and forwards between them forever?"

I answered that if he could start it, and get out of the way of the light beam quickly enough, I would keep it going.

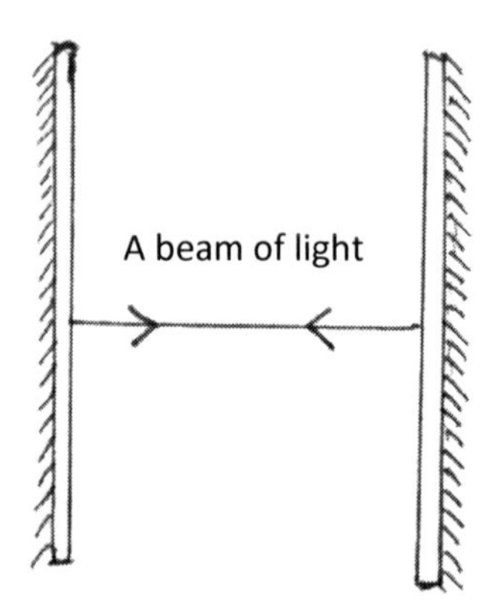

Technology's triumph

Chacha, who was quite sceptical about scientific research, once said to me, "Who knows, scientists might turn out to have been completely mistaken about electricity. Maybe they'll discover that it's completely different to what they thought."

"You needn't worry about it, Chacha," I comforted him. "The television will still carry on working!"

"In which case, I don't care!" Chacha sighed with relief.

Faster than light

I once told Chacha that light travels much faster than sound. "Don't be silly!" he retorted. "When I switch on the TV, I hear the sound *before* I see the picture!"

Beyond our ken

Imagine a story, in which the word God does not appear, and which is written in such a way that the whole text itself takes the shape of the letters G-O-D. Perhaps our universe is like this. The more minutely we inspect it, the harder it is to see God.

Where is God? God is everywhere.

What God is not

I believe that to call someone a philosopher certainly amounts to praise, since a philosopher is commonly thought of as a wise person, trying to fathom the mysteries of the Universe.

On the contrary, however, to call God a philosopher is certainly derogatory. God has infinite wisdom and knows all; He sees things to their logical conclusions instantaneously, without having to go through any intervening logical steps. To call God a philosopher would be to deny these attributes of Him. Therefore, even though I don't know what God is, I certainly know what God is not!

Praise be to God,
who, in His infinite wisdom,
is not a philosopher!

A finely tuned organ

Lungs are one of the most marvellous gifts of God. Their structural intricacy is mind-boggling, which is just as well, in view of the fact that they have to deal with every single blood cell individually. An average person contains about 5 to 6 litres of blood, and each cubic millimetre contains 5 to 6 million blood cells.

How does each blood cell get its share of oxygen, and filter out any toxic waste? Only the lungs can carry out such a stupendous task so efficiently, even though they are already challenged by environmental pollution on a grand scale.

There are 350 million *alveoli* (bubble-like air sacs) in each lung. Around each alveolus is a network of microscopic blood vessels, called capillaries. Capillaries are so small that when blood eventually passes through them, the blood cells – too small to be seen by the human eye – have to move in *single file*. It is here that gas exchange takes place. To maximize gas exchange, the lungs provide a tennis-court-sized area packed into the volume of the chest.

How does this exchange take place? Oxygen from the air inside the lungs seeps through the one-cell thick walls of the capillaries into the blood, turning its colour from dark to bright red. Carbon dioxide passes the opposite way. The lining of each alveolus is incredibly thin, coated with a film of moisture in which gases can dissolve.

What makes the lungs truly one of the greatest marvels of Nature is the fact that the blood purified by the lungs not only sustains and repairs the rest of the body but also sustains and repairs the lungs themselves! How does it come about that the lungs are wired up *to themselves* for this purpose? In other words, how does the blood nourish and sustain the very capillaries where the blood cells themselves travel in single file in order to be individually oxygenated?

Our lungs not only bring about gas exchange, to support our bodies and brains, but they support our general well-being. The therapeutic effects of lungs are tremendous. Through yawning and deep breathing exercises, lungs contribute tremendously to help us overcome anxiety, and enhance our health, happiness and serenity. They give us such important human traits as speech, singing and laughter. We cannot even enjoy a good joke without strong and healthy lungs!

Even the apparently simple process of coughing is much more complicated than it seems. It is a dual-purpose mechanism, ejecting unwanted material inhaled from the outside as soon as it enters the wind-pipe, and also ejecting unwanted material that builds up in the lungs. How the lungs breathe in and breathe out is yet another story.

However, our lungs are only able to cope with a certain amount of toxins, not with a persistent onslaught. They already have to meet the challenges that arise from smoke in the atmosphere, but at least this smoke does have some form of justification in terms of the technology which gives rise to it.

But why should anyone voluntarily burden their lungs with cigarette smoke as well? Our lungs should be regarded as the precious gift that they are. Indeed, looking after our lungs is one way of showing our love of Nature, and to fail to take proper care is to show disrespect to Nature – which has given us all we have.

The pursuit of happiness

We are all in pursuit of happiness, yet we know neither what it is nor how to achieve it. We have discovered to our great disappointment that health, wealth and knowledge are causally unrelated to happiness – you may have them all and still be unhappy. Happiness is a much more subtle thing.

But surely happiness is easier for a religious person, who can understand it as a gift of God. God is all-wise, all-knowing, all-powerful, all-kind. He can do what no other can. He has created us, knows us intimately, even to the number of fundamental particles which constitute us, and in what configuration they are arranged. He is the greatest of all doctors, and knows all the needs of His creations. Therefore, if God is with you, who can harm you? So, for people who believe in God and honour Him, there is no need to worry, either here or in the life hereafter. Their happiness is inevitable!

Did you know?

People in Australia use their umbrellas upside down. Why? Because in Australia, it rains upside down.

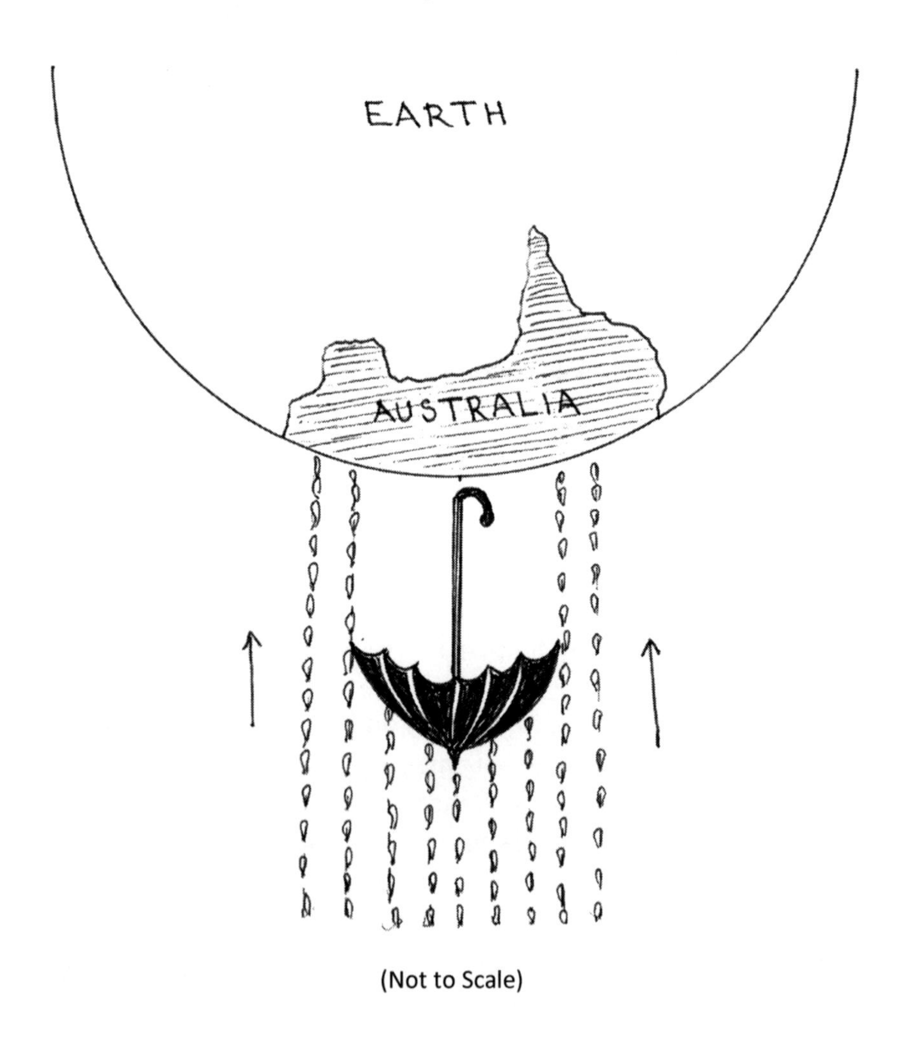

(Not to Scale)

Investment in eternal life

For theists, life in this world – which hardly ever lasts more than a hundred years – is merely a stepping-stone to the next. There is eternal life after our apparent death, and what we do in this life to serve our neighbours determines what will happen to us in the next.

How does it come about, then, that many theists still devote almost all of their time to pursuits which are self-serving, which are strictly of this world and have no positive bearing on life in the hereafter? There is so much at stake! Yet they continue to go for the short-term gains of this world, while ignoring the eternal gains which, if they would only seek them, would be waiting for them in the next. Should they not try their best to rise above such short-sighted irrationality?

Three questions in the theology of sin

- Will we be punished by God for the sins committed by us only in our thoughts and dreams? If so, then I am afraid Heaven will remain totally deserted. If not, then such pleasures need not be avoided, and lucky are those who have fertile imaginations!
- There are sins we regret having committed. Are there any sins we regret having not committed?
- Should people who commit no sin and go to Heaven envy those who, after leading a life full of pleasurable sin, repent at the last moment and come to Heaven all the same?

A God's-eye view

God can view a given scene simultaneously from all possible angles. We know, however, that if we ourselves were to superimpose all the views of a given scene, we would end up with no view at all. So what is God's point of view?

A sad reflection

Chacha was one day feeling grim about the philosophical development of humans.

"We know nothing when we are born," he said. "We begin by taking things for granted. We appear to know more and more as we advance in our life. Then we start becoming more and more sceptical about what we believed we knew. Eventually, we know that we know nothing at all, and die."

An idea that changed mankind

Einstein before thinking of the Theory of Relativity

Einstein after thinking of the Theory of Relativity

Everyday Ethics

Everyday Ethics

"Don't talk to strangers"

Chacha said that when he was very young he would wander around without any concern. No one ever warned him about the dangers of strangers.

"We kids came to no harm!" he said. "Has the world only just become bad? Or has it been bad for centuries, and we've only just discovered the fact?"

Reasons for sensitivities

It is certainly true that we ought to respect other people's feelings and sensitivities, regardless of why they are sensitive. If a person is deeply hurt whenever you wiggle your ears, you ought not to do it in front of them. It's not much of a loss to you, I hope.

The situation becomes more complicated, however, when respecting a person's feelings entails that your own feelings become hurt in the process. In these cases, we end up considering who has the better reason for their sensitivity.

If someone's sensitivities are based on superstitions, or mistaken beliefs, and yours are based on rationality and common sense, would you and ought you still to respect their feelings at the expense of your own?

An honest man's honesty

Suppose a man is speeding when he drives past a speed-camera, but somehow his misdemeanour goes undetected. Rather than celebrate his luck, he drives on to the police station and pays the appropriate speeding fine of his own accord. Chacha called this 'being honest' rather than merely naïve. Was Chacha being honest or merely naïve?

Chacha and the tonga-wala

A *tonga-wala* was beckoning passengers to his *tonga* – a horse-driven cart, which could carry four passengers: "Two rupees to Saddar Bazaar, two rupees, two rupees!"

Chacha got on, but the tonga-wala kept beckoning to others for some time. When he realised that no other passengers were interested, he started shouting: "One rupee to Saddar Bazaar, one rupee, one rupee!" This attracted three more passengers, and the tonga set off.

When they arrived at Saddar Bazaar, the tonga-wala asked the other passengers for one rupee each, and asked Chacha to pay two rupees.

"Why charge me more than the others?" Chacha queried.

The tonga-wala tried to justify himself by saying, "Don't you remember, Baba ji, I'd settled on two rupees with you?"

Chacha became very upset, and he did not know what to do, until he noticed a policeman who happened to be patrolling the area. Chacha beckoned him over.

The policeman heard the story from both parties, and said to Chacha, "Baba ji, don't waste your time on that one. Just give him two rupees and get on with what you came here to do. Leave it to me to sort him out!"

Chacha was pleased to hear this from the sympathetic policeman, and immediately took his advice by handing over the two rupees to the tonga-wala and leaving.

As Chacha was going away, he stopped when he heard the policeman start to berate the tonga-wala. Turning round, he was just in time to see the two rupees being confiscated by the policeman, and pocketed.

But Chacha was pleased. In effect, he had paid the policeman two rupees to sort out the rogue tonga-wala, and the ride itself was free! Was Chacha being naïve again, or not?

A tonga

A free lunch

Moriarty Junior, the master thief, goes into a vegetable store to get some food for his lunch. Next to the display, a local blind man is resting in a chair, waiting for the shopkeeper to return from a back room. The blind man has nothing to do with the shop or its owner.

Moriarty takes advantage of the shopkeeper's absence, and of the seated man's blindness, to steal some potatoes and cauliflower. Then he quickly leaves the store.

Clearly, he stole from the shopkeeper, but not from the blind man. He also deceived the shopkeeper. But did he in any way deceive the blind man?

An affair to remember

Suppose Alan and Betty have been married for the past two years. Betty has been perfectly happy in the marriage but then discovers that Alan has been having an affair over the same period. Has she been harmed?

If so, do you believe that the harm has been taking place over the whole of the two-year period, or that it started only after the horrendous discovery?

If the harm occurred only *after* the discovery, then this would suggest that it was the discovery that was harmful, and not the affair!

On the other hand, if the harm started at the beginning of the affair, what *kind* of harm was it that Betty sustained over the two-year period, bearing in mind that she was perfectly happy during that time? And what if she discovers that Alan had not been unfaithful after all? Would the harm spanning the two years suddenly disappear into thin air?

Dreams are dreams

We're not in control of our dreams – but we are in control of what we say about them. We often dream about our friends and relatives when we sleep. Is it ever unethical to recount these dreams to them?

Beneath the surface

Can you find out from a person's physical behaviour alone whether the person is moral or not? Two men could both claim to be conscientious objectors, and refuse to go to war, but while one is motivated by his moral standards, the other is simply scared for his life.

For any given good deed, we can imagine an underlying motive that shows it to be morally vacuous, or even wrong. Do you think it's possible that a person could do nothing but good throughout his life, but still be immoral due to his motives?

Doing the donkey work

Good motives are not always enough. A lot of harm can be done for the best of motives. Even assuming our motives to be laudable, our methods are not always the best for achieving our ends.

A man was once riding his donkey with a sack of flour resting in front of him. He realised at some point that the donkey was having to struggle hard, going uphill under such a weight, and out of pity he decided to lighten the donkey's burden.

To this end, and while continuing to ride, he took the sack off the donkey and put it on his own head. The donkey thanked him with bulging eyes for being so thoughtful and kind-hearted a master.

An imaginary misfortune

In order to tell a lie, one needs some imagination. Unfortunately, some people are lacking in this mental ability. So, although telling lies is bad, not being *able* to tell one is a misfortune!

Excuse me sir, but...

If I asked you whether in general you ought to do something quite simple to help a stranger in need, I am quite sure you would say yes. Now consider the following simple situation, in which you could help a stranger with hardly any effort at all.

You see a stranger in a restaurant, who has some remnant of foodstuff hanging in his beard, of which he is oblivious. Surely it ought to be a simple matter to save the man from a day's ridicule. But how would you go about it?

Would you try to dislodge the item by secretly flicking it off the man's beard, while his mind is on something else? Would you be courageous enough to tell him openly about the state of his beard? Or is there any other strategy you can think of?

Marital bliss

The reader is invited to try to arrange the following marital scenarios in order of moral severity, in the light of their own moral views:

- A man cheats on his wife, and she doesn't find out.
- A man cheats on his wife, and she does find out – and so *she* starts cheating on *him*.
- A man cheats on his wife, and she merely *suspects* that he has, so she starts cheating on him.
- A man does *not* cheat on his wife, but she *suspects* that he has, so she starts cheating on him.
- A man mistakenly suspects that his wife is cheating on him, so he starts cheating on her. His wife finds out, and so she starts cheating on him.
- A man and his wife each mistakenly suspect the other of cheating, and so they both start cheating on each other.

An unwilling doorman

As I left a shopping mall one day, I held the door open for the customer behind me. But as he passed through, another person came along behind him, and I continued to hold the door for her too. The situation progressed quickly. Before I knew it, lo and behold, a steady stream of people were coming through, none of them electing to take the door from my hands, to pass on to others in the usual way! Some giggled, some kept both hands in their pockets, some muttered thanks, but most were completely oblivious to the service I was providing! I was stuck, obliged to keep hold of the heavy swing door, so as to prevent harm to the others.

While this was going on, I felt very embarrassed. But thinking about it now, I ask myself why this should have been so. Who should be embarrassed – the one being helpful, or the ones being helped, and unappreciatively benefiting from my predicament?

An unwilling donor

Suppose I need £1,000 for urgent medical treatment, but I'm broke. As I am a deserving case, my friend would be only too happy to offer this money if I asked it of him. However, I have not yet asked him, and furthermore I don't know about his willingness – indeed, I believe my friend would refuse me the money. For this reason, rather than asking him, I instead *rob* my friend of £1,000!

Ought my friend to take exception to this? After all, he was willing to give me the cash. His charitableness existed even while I was stealing from him! What's the difference?

Accidental innocence

Suppose one day a man buys a newspaper, and on his way out of the shop he spots a good book on display next to the newspapers. As he leaves, he secretly grabs and pockets the book.

However, on arriving home, he makes the embarrassing discovery that the book came *free* with that day's paper anyway! Did he or did he not steal the book? Did he commit any crime, moral or legal? And did it make sense for him to continue to feel guilty?

A good joke can be bad

Some jokes are plainly in bad taste. But even a good-hearted joke – even one that your audience will deeply appreciate – can be thoroughly unethical to tell.

Despite what some say, laughter isn't always the best medicine. If you don't want to upset the serenity of a very heavy smoker, you'd better not tell them a good joke. When Chacha's asthma was really bad, I was usually thoughtful enough not to tell him my best jokes.

The rebirth of a loved one

It is a sad fact that we tend not to appreciate properly those relatives and friends we have with us all the time – until they die. Only then do we start to realise how valuable and important they were to us. But by then it is too late to alter the way we behaved towards them.

We know that eventually our relatives and friends will die. But merely considering this possibility is not enough to make us realise in advance how much they mean to us, and therefore treat them better. Yet after we discover that the person is dead, our relationship with them improves dramatically! If only there was a way of making deaths temporary, these relationships could be resumed in their improved states.

This effect could be achieved if a person received a false report of a loved one's demise. If I received a mistaken report that my friend had died, I would feel exactly as I would have felt had he really died. It would prompt me to realise how good a friend he was, and to think of how I could have better appreciated his company. Then, when I discover that the report is false, it would be as though he had been reborn, and I would cherish his friendship even more. It is the *belief* that the report is true that matters, not its actual truth.

It looks as though we have begun to make out a case for deliberately giving people convincing but false reports of their loved ones' deaths!

Last wishes

Why do we regard it as important to honour promises once made to those now dead? It seems that the importance we attach to such a commitment does not depend upon religious faith. Atheists, and those who lose their faith, feel compelled to honour these promises.

Some mothers do 'ave 'em

You're walking in the park with your elderly mother when it starts pouring down with rain. There's a shelter nearby – would you run off to it straightaway, and watch while your mother arrives in her own time? Or would you continue to walk with her?

Notice that by staying with your mother you cannot prevent both her and yourself from getting wet. But you can keep *yourself* dry, if you wish, by rushing to the shelter. Isn't one wet person better than two?

The purely rational choice might be to abandon your mother to the elements. But if you were to do this, would any onlookers regard you with approval? Perhaps more to the point, what would your mother think?

Love for humanity

None of us enjoy thinking about our own inevitable demise. When we do think about it, we often try to convince ourselves that the prospect isn't so bad after all. Which of the following two thoughts is more comforting?

- "All of us will eventually die."
- "Even though I'll die, others will continue to live."

I suspect that the first thought is more comforting for most people. If so, whatever happened to our love for humanity?

The green-eyed monster

Jealousy has a strange effect: rather than encouraging us to do better than the person of whom we are jealous, it encourages us to make that person worse off! We would have it that neither person is well-off, rather than both.

I suppose this effect – and jealousy itself – arises out of simple competition. Jealousy is debilitating to our health and happiness, and this kind of competition doesn't help in any way. Our aim should be to run ahead, not to push others back!

Choosing love

Betty loves Alan very much, but he does not love her back. If Alan died, Betty would be much more upset than Alan would be if she died.

Unfortunately, both Alan and Betty have been victimised by an evil tyrant who, out of pure viciousness, is going to execute just one of them. He leaves the decision up to you as to which.

All other things being equal, there will be less suffering caused if Betty dies rather than Alan. If you select Alan, you are willingly bringing about more suffering than was necessary. But if you select Betty, you are punishing the more loving of the two.

So, who stays and who goes?

Supporting elders

When I was walking in the local countryside, I saw two trees, one on either side of a stream. The image struck me, because one tree appeared to be leaning against the other!

Apparently, an old tree had fallen down, and as it was falling it had been 'caught' by a younger tree standing on the other side of the stream. You might be impressed by the altruistic behaviour of the younger tree, which was now supporting the old one day in, day out. But of course the younger one, being rooted to the spot, had no choice in the matter, and had been unable to get out of the way.

You might think that the position of a person is quite different from the young tree, in that he can always elect not to act as a support for anyone else. Not so. Our morality acts upon us like roots, holding us in position, preventing us from acting differently than we do. Should we regret our moral roots as a loss of freedom, or should we welcome them as the gift of our true moral selves?

Painful life or none at all?

There will come a time when there is no more life left anywhere in the Universe. This vision of a completely inanimate universe is incredibly bleak and horrific.

Compare this universe to one full of life, but where that life has nothing but suffering. Which universe is better?

A pain no longer felt?

If a person has suffered a lot of pain – perhaps from a long drawn out disease, or from terrible circumstances – we feel their pain even after it has gone. Perhaps they escaped the cause, or perhaps they are now dead because they didn't. Either way, the pain is no longer felt by them – but, strangely, passes on to us! Why do we feel pain about a pain no longer felt?

A generous helping

Chacha, my father, was pleasantly naïve and had many other good qualities. Though totally illiterate, he was appreciative of education. And though very poor, he was generous and kind-hearted.

One of my uncles, unlike Chacha, was quite well-off – a bearded and religious man, who had been a high-ranking officer in the Pakistan Navy, at a time when Chacha had been only a humble, low-ranking civilian cook in the Army. Uncle once visited us to attend a hearing at a local court, and asked Chacha to go with him. Chacha felt elated to have been asked to keep Uncle company, and happily went with him to the court.

The hearing was delayed, and my uncle took Chacha to a nearby restaurant for some tea. Chacha had never before visited such a grand restaurant, never having been able to afford such a luxury. It was an open-air restaurant, and customers sat under a canopy by the footpath on the roadside. The waiter came and left their tea and a large tray laden with snacks. There were *samosas*, *burfi*, and some very expensive cakes.

The custom in the restaurant was that you paid only for what you ate. But Chacha didn't know this. He thought that Uncle would have to pay for everything on the tray, whether eaten or not, and he was impressed by the size of what he took to be Uncle's order. Uncle took a single slice of cake, and Chacha hesitatingly helped himself to another.

When they had finished their tea and while they were getting ready to leave, Chacha was concerned about the uneaten snacks that remained on the plate, particularly the expensive cakes. As Uncle would have to pay for them all, it seemed wrong to give them back to the restaurant, for possible resale. So, to Uncle's surprise, Chacha started beckoning to the beggars, young and old, who were near the restaurant. Uncle's surprise turned into horror when Chacha, taking his approval for granted, started giving each beggar a snack from the 'leftovers' on the tray.

Beads of perspiration appeared on Uncle's forehead as he thought of the expense that was fast building up, particularly when the expensive cakes were being gobbled up by the beggars in front of him. He could not stop the beggars from accepting what they were offered. And he didn't feel able to ask Chacha to desist, for Chacha had always thought very highly of Uncle, and Chacha's esteem was more important to Uncle than the expense of this generosity. In fact, Uncle's prestige and honour in the village depended in part on Chacha's good opinion of him.

Chacha, however, oblivious to all this, pursued his charitable work with gusto, while my uncle could only look on agog, quickly coming to regret that he had taken no more than one slice of cake for himself before the general distribution started! Chacha's excitement was not over until he had emptied the whole tray.

Sign of a good businessman?

A friend of mine called Karim was a self-employed sign-writer. He had a unique way of giving estimates to his customers. After listening to a customer's requirements, he would orally quote a figure to test the ground. How he continued would depend upon the customer's first reaction. If the customer seemed quite happy, Karim would slip in: "Plus materials." If, on the other hand, the customer raised his eyebrows or reacted negatively in any way, Karim would immediately add: "This, *of course*, *includes* all materials!"

A full refund

I once ordered some books for £25 from an online bookstore. They were sent promptly and my account was appropriately debited. However, the parcel was lost in transit, together with its accompanying invoice. When I complained to the store, they sent me a replacement packet with an invoice for £0.00. This invoice showed me that the store was aware that I had already paid the £25 cost of the books. So far so good. I was pleased with the prompt customer service.

But the books turned out to be not to my liking. I therefore returned them in the same packing, together with the £0.00 invoice, the only one I had. The store e-mailed me, confirming that it had received the books back for refund, and that my account had been credited with the full £0.00. Not so good.

Intentions and consequences

The person who tries to do good is better than the person who tries to do harm. Also, the person who *accidentally* does good is better than the person who *accidentally* does harm.

So who is better: the person who tries to do good but accidentally does harm, or the person who tries to do harm but accidentally does good?

Unnatural ethical systems

Our natural instincts are the result of millions of years of evolution. The more our morality approximates with these instincts, the more practicable it becomes.

History is witness that even the death penalty – by beheading, burning at the stake, stoning to death, and many other gruesome executions – has been unsuccessful in enforcing an idea of morality that was in direct conflict with our natural instincts. Lovers from many eras and parts of the world have suffered from punishments such as these.

Today, in the West, adults are relatively free to express their love for each other. It seems as though life in the West is closer to nature. Some would say that it runs more smoothly and happily as a result.

Deceptively beautiful

Case 1

Does it make any sense to wear a wig or make-up in the presence of a friend who knows you well, and has seen you without it? If so, why so?

Case 2

Is it not morally equivalent to a lie, if, by the use of a wig or make-up, you make a stranger believe that you are what in fact you are not? If not, why not?

A free riding logician

A volcano erupts, and lava is flowing directly towards a petrol station. It will reach the station in about two hours and, when it does, all the petrol will explode.

A logician from the local university comes across this scene on his way home by car. By coincidence, he is fairly low on petrol – so he pulls in, quickly fills his tank, and then departs without paying. "After all," he reasons, "the fuel will all go up in smoke in a couple of hours anyway. Isn't it better that I put some of it to use before this happens? I know it would make a difference to the owner if I paid rather than didn't, but those aren't the right choices to compare. The right comparison is between *taking* and *not taking*. I'll either take the petrol without paying, or I won't take it at all. Whichever I do, the owner won't get money for it, so it makes no difference to him either way. Therefore, it's better I take the petrol."

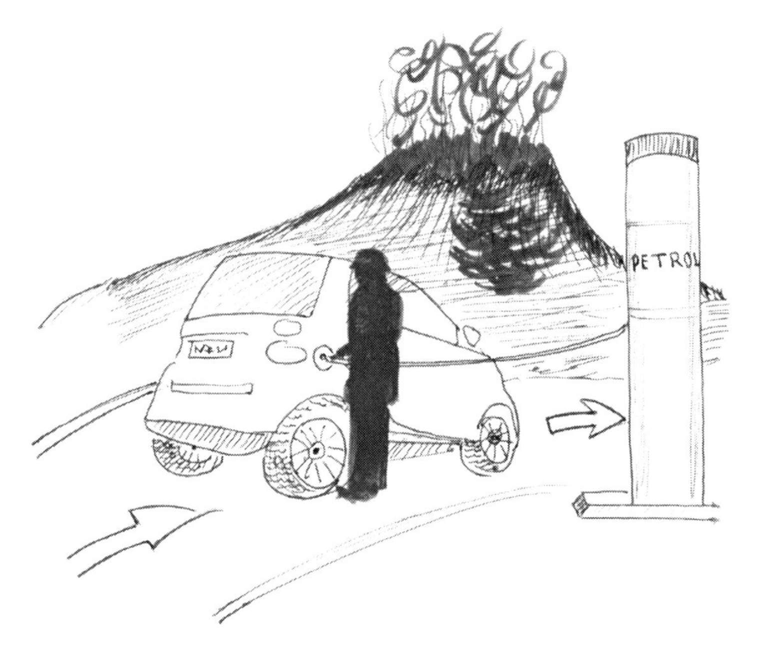

Was this theft? Ought the man to have paid for the petrol, even though the whole lot was about to disappear anyway?

When he arrives home he boasts to a friend about his free petrol. It turns out that his friend bought some petrol at the same station earlier that afternoon, just after the eruption – but he had paid.

The logician's friend hears the arguments and is convinced. "But this is grossly unfair!" he says furiously. "There's no difference between my petrol and yours. So why should I have had to pay? I'd better be quick if I'm going to get a refund."

An ill-defined reaction

If we discover that a friend has had a painful illness, but has just recovered from it, does rationality require us to be more sad about the illness or more happy about the recovery? If you think you could be both, how is it that you could be happy and sad at the same time?

To pee or not to pee

There are some things you can do *without* permission which you cannot do *with* permission. For example, peeing behind a tree might be ignored by a policeman. But if the policeman were asked for permission he would not give it.

Regretting regretting

I once found Chacha looking unhappy. He seemed uneasy about something. When I enquired, he said, "The other day I did a good deed, and gave ten pounds to someone in trouble. However, I later on realised that I needed the money myself, and regretted giving it away. So now my troubles are twofold. Not only have I lost the ten pounds, but by regretting my charity I have lost any moral benefit it might have earned me. So now I regret regretting it."

Can it be ethical to be slightly unethical in order to be greatly more ethical?

If you make a promise to a friend, you might come to realise that keeping the promise will harm him. For example, you promise to lend him your car whenever it's available, but one night he asks while drunk. In this case, you might decide to be slightly unethical – by breaking your promise – in order to be greatly more ethical – by preventing an accident. Would this be ethical? Are there any promises which must *never* be broken?

The ultimate status of morals

When God first dictated the rules of behaviour for mankind, how did He decide what they should be?

God couldn't have referred to some idea of morality already present, because this would mean that God Himself was subject to a pre-existing moral framework. This is plainly absurd, as God is both above and prior to everything.

So God must have written the rules Himself. In which case, the rules of behaviour are not really *moral* rules at all, they are just *God's* rules. If He had wanted, He could have chosen otherwise: He could have made giving to charity wrong and killing innocents right!

Since morality comes from God, He is not accountable to anyone or anything for His deeds. So who knows, He could very well send all the sinners to Heaven and all the saintly ones to Hell! What difference would it make to Him?

God is all-powerful, and He could do this if He wanted. But true believers need not worry. With peace of mind, they can rely on their belief in God's all-kindness, and can trust that God will always use His infinite power in the best way.

The Big Brother Experience

The Big Brother Experience

For 2 to 3 months each year since the year 2000, up to 20 or so people allow themselves to be put together into a house which is specially constructed so that they can be filmed as they go about their day to day activities. The result is shown on national television for long hours each day and night under the title *Big Brother*, and this reality show is watched by some 8 million viewers.

Each week one or more of the participants (the 'housemates') are eliminated from the show. Usually, a secret vote among the housemates results in a shortlist, and the viewers choose from this who is to go. The elimination continues until just one housemate is left, and this survivor receives the prize, £100,000 in 2007, plus all the benefits of the resulting publicity. Indeed all the contestants receive a great deal of publicity, not always positive.

Each year a long selection process is followed to determine who the lucky (or unlucky) people are to be, and even though I have not appeared in the program, I am in the position of being able to give some insight into this process from beginning to end. My knowledge of the process comes from having gone through it.

My decision to audition

I have never been an avid fan of *Big Brother*. But my children watched it a fair amount, and I must have seen it a number of times in passing. The only occasions on which I watched for any length of time were when the Indian film star Shilpa Shetty was appearing in a Celebrity Big Brother series very early in 2007.

My ignorance of the program is one reason why it is so surprising to me now that I very nearly appeared in it. The knowledge of the program that I have since acquired is one reason why I now believe myself to have had a lucky escape. But in early 2007 it seemed to me that there were many possible advantages to appearing, and not the least of these seemed to be that the publication of this present book, *The Logic of Half a Moustache*, would be greatly facilitated.

A surprising queue

3 February 07

After Shilpa Shetty's appearance on *Big Brother*, my son Mahboob suggested to me that I would enjoy appearing in it myself, and he told me that auditions for the next *Big Brother* series were going to take place very soon. I discovered when and where I needed to go, and a frosty morning in February saw me rise at 5am and catch an early train to attend the first audition in Manchester.

In my naïvety I had expected to be drinking coffee in New Century House by 9am, and home again by mid-afternoon. But I had no idea what was going to be involved. My first impression when I arrived at New Century House was mind-boggling, and I was totally unprepared for the sea of people I found queuing outside – mostly very young and in all sorts of theatrical costumes, drastically made up to attract attention. I, on the other hand, at 62 years old, was among the oldest contestants, and I was dressed just as usual, in my ordinary shirt, jacket and trousers. Also, as far as I could tell, I was the only Asian there. I soon felt myself to be very much out of place.

Nevertheless I stood at the end of the pavement-wide queue, rapidly growing behind me as I walked, and I followed it around block after block of buildings for what seemed like miles, and for a long time thought I would have no chance of getting to the front. As time went on I felt more and more inclined to flee the scene and make my way back to Bradford. However, my family knew where I had come, and I was committed to the present course by my unwillingness to lose face.

While I was queuing, one of the other contestants nearby caught my attention. He was announcing to everyone that he had already been to the previous auditions just held in Newcastle. Despite his lack of success, he was able to tell us what to expect, at least at this first stage. His suit was in dazzling gold, he wore a tall black top hat with wide brim, and, at his other end, double length shiny black shoes. I listened carefully to the free advice this guru was giving to those near him, but if anything he increased my unease. Certainly it was too late for me to dress any differently.

The initial cull

The queue was not as slow-moving as you might have supposed, and after about an hour and a half I entered New Century House, where the sea of people continued to flow. As each new wave of people came through the door, they were ushered forward onto four floodlit platforms, 10 to 15 people on each, to take part in group activities. So 4 groups, about 50 people, were assessed every 10 minutes or so, with only 2 people chosen from each group to go forward to further tests. This brutal annihilation of the majority was hit and miss, but it was required if the number of applicants was to be reduced to manageable proportions.

Because of my age, I was very apprehensive about the group activities. I was not worried about my fitness, for although 62 years old I was a regular jogger. Nor was I worried about my intelligence, for throughout my life I have always kept my mind as exercised as my body. My worry was that some of the requirements of the assessment would be lost on me, due to the generation gap and the cultural divide between myself and the other applicants, who were for the most part young and natives of this country.

A further problem arose because I couldn't understand the Liverpudlian accent of some of the group of young people who seemed to be adopting me. I tried to hang back, so that I could join another group, but I was continually urged forward. If I couldn't properly hear what was being said I wouldn't be able to interact successfully with the others in my group. To improve my chances, I tried to learn what I could of this new language while we waited, but with no success; and in the end, what I had feared would happen did happen – I was called on stage to take part in group activities with people I could hardly understand!

However, things didn't go as badly as I had feared. Each platform had a 'facilitator', and I was pleasantly surprised when our own facilitator introduced a discussion about Shilpa Shetty, and whether she had been a victim of racism in *Big Brother*. My view is that claims about racism are generally exaggerated, and I expressed this view.

The other task given to us by our facilitator was to pair up and tell our partners all about ourselves. When time was up, we were to report our findings to the group.

I found myself paired with a charming punk rocker with brightly coloured hair that pointed up to the ceiling. I am afraid that, although I told her a great deal about myself, there was not much time left in which to learn a lot about her, before the facilitator shouted: "Time's up! Get together. Quick!"

My partner was able to tell the group quite a lot about me, but when it came to my turn to describe her I was only able to say that I had met her in the queue, and I didn't know her name. The facilitator asked me what I liked most about her, and I said, "I like her hair!" People seemed to find this quite amusing.

When we had all finished, the facilitator took a little while to make up his mind. Then he asked us all to put out our right hands. He was going to stamp the lucky contestants with a *Big Brother* seal, as proof that they had qualified for the next round. He looked at me and stamped my hand first, and then that of another lady I had met in the queue. He asked the others to go home, including my unlucky activities partner, and the man in the golden suit.

Questions, questions

I and the other winner were escorted to the next stage of the audition. We were shown into another large hall, where we joined all the other pairs who had so far passed their initial audition. They were all frantically attacking a 10-page questionnaire.

My photograph was taken and stuck on the front of one such questionnaire, and I was asked to fill it in. There were perhaps 100 questions to answer, some of them calling for much detailed explanation, and it took me some 2 hours to complete.

I first of all had to read through the detailed instructions, and warnings about the need for accuracy. This concern with accuracy was evidenced by the fact that many of the questions occurred more than once, though in a different form. The various answers could easily be used as a check on the candidate's consistency.

Most of the questions were about me and how I think about myself. Some were about how I think about other people, and sought presumably to discover how I would relate to others in the *Big Brother* house. And other questions related to what I thought about the program itself.

I dived in enthusiastically, determined to do myself justice. Among the many questions were the following.

Q. What are you gaining from the auditions?
A. I am rediscovering myself. The experience is teaching me the value of 'be yourself', a simple key to success in life.

Q. What annoys you most?
A. A BMW left blocking my drive.

Q. What would you do if you won the National Lottery?
A. Nothing, for a while.

Q. What is your outlook on life?
A. I am a humanist.

Q. What kind of action do you find most despicable?
A. Cruelty to a child.

Q. Would you ever prefer Hell to Heaven?
A. Yes, if Heaven were crowded with those who have killed the innocent in the name of God.

Q. What kind of people like you?
A. Everyone likes me, except my close relatives.

The questions went on and on. When I finally finished, there was a long wait before I was given a 5 minute filmed audition, in which I was asked further questions. In the course of answering, I admitted that I had found the *Big Brother* program quite boring and said that it needed something to liven it up. I had in mind that watching people sleep was not very interesting. The parts of the celebrity season I had watched had certainly not given me any idea of the true extent of the horrors of life in the *Big Brother* house.

I was asked for the names of those I had found boring, but was unable to supply any, as, apart from Shilpa Shetty, all those appearing in the celebrity series had been new to me, and I just couldn't remember who they were. Perhaps if they had been less boring I would have remembered their names. All I could say was that there were quite a few.

The questionnaire had elicited the fact of my literary pursuits and that, as well as having written a book in Urdu, I was in the process of writing one in English, called *The Logic of Half a Moustache*. So they asked me about the title, and I was able to give them the details of the corresponding item in this present book. But of course I was unable to tell them about *The Big Brother Experience*.

I then waited perhaps another 15 minutes until I was escorted to another hall, which was almost full, and I realised that the filmed audition must have gone well enough. I was given yet another questionnaire, this time 40 pages long, and told I had as long as I wanted to complete the task. I was told I should also come back on the Monday for a further 10-minute audition.

I was advised that, when I had finished the questionnaire and departed, I should avoid any journalists who might be outside the building. If they were impossible to avoid, I should lie and tell them that I had been rejected. This advice led me to think that maybe there was a chance I would be successful, and I began to take the selection process much more seriously.

There were 2 to 3 hundred questions to answer, and unlike many other candidates, who told me they were missing out some of the questions, I answered every one. The questions were probing and designed to give a complete picture of the candidates. They asked me about every aspect of my life, public and private, from childhood to the present.

As with the first questionnaire I was determined to be perfectly frank in the answers I gave, and I dived in again. Two hours and fifty questions later I was still writing...

Q. Who do you think you most resemble?
A. Omar Sharif, the actor from *Lawrence of Arabia*.

Q. When is the magic of sunset the greatest?
A. When viewed in the company of a beautiful woman you're in love with.

After another two hours, hunger and thirst were attacking, and the questions were becoming more and more exhaustive and more and more exhausting...

Q. How do you deal with insults?
A. I can take argument or insults in my stride, so long as there is no physical contact – hot air doesn't hurt!

All the other candidates had long gone, and the lady waiting at the desk was looking glum. It was she who had told me to take as long as I needed.

Q. Draw yourself in the space provided.
A.

Another hour, another thousand questions...

Q. What would you like to change about *Big Brother*?
A. This questionnaire!

At about 11pm I finished. I decided to ignore the optional sheet which asked for any additional information I might want to give, and set off for home. New Century House was almost empty when I left, and fortunately no journalists were still waiting in the cold outside, so I wasn't obliged to lie to them about what had taken place.

I arrived home at nearly 1am, and my family was anxiously waiting for me. When I looked at my hand I saw that the *Big Brother* stamp was still there. It took a lot of washing to remove.

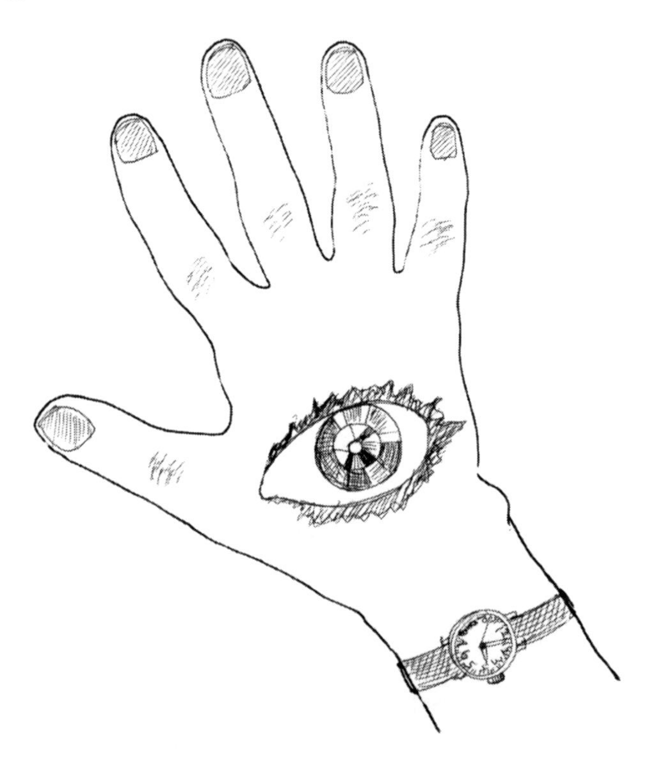

Big Sister

5 February 07

On Monday I returned to Manchester for the further audition. There were no crowds as there had been on the Saturday. I had been given a pass to allow me into New Century House.

When my number was called, I was taken into a room containing a chair surrounded by a black curtain. This was an attempt to recreate the atmosphere of the *Big Brother* Diary Room used in the program. I was asked to leave my coat and belongings outside the curtain and to go though and sit on the chair.

The voice of Big Brother (in this case, female!) welcomed me through the curtain and then asked me questions. She asked me in particular how I thought I might be able to contribute to *Big Brother*. I said that I hoped to inject humour into the program, and to raise the cultural issues to which my background gave me special access.

My replies to questions two days earlier had in many cases been fairly philosophical and, on being asked about this, I now said that what was important about a philosophical attitude was a willingness to suppose anything to be the case, for the sake of argument. A philosopher should take nothing for granted and should develop the habit of mind of questioning his own beliefs.

Being asked about my humanist attitude to life, I said that much of the strife in the world has been, and is, due to religious differences. If we concentrated on our common humanity, rather than these differences, the world would be a better place. I quoted Bertrand Russell's: "Remember your humanity and forget the rest."

Ms Big Brother concluded by saying, "Thank you *very much*, Mahmud," and I left her presence.

I then made my way back to Bradford. My feeling was that the interview had not gone well. I had been suffering from a cold which was affecting my hearing, and I'd had to ask for a number of questions to be repeated.

After arriving home I had to wait – not just a few days, as I had hoped – but about 7 weeks, before I heard the result of my Manchester auditions. Meantime, the strain of waiting made it difficult to engage properly in my normal activities.

On looking at the *Big Brother* website I found the following announcement:

> **Applications for *Big Brother* are closed**
> **Wednesday 14 February**
> Day 35, 11:31
>
> Thousands of you applied for *Big Brother* 2007...
>
> *Big Brother* 2007 applications are now closed. Big Brother is currently eyeing over thousands of applicants to find housemates this summer. If you've got through to the next round, Big Brother will contact you shortly.
>
> Good luck, and remember, Big Brother is always watching...

22 March 07

I was contacted by *Big Brother* on 22nd March and told that I had been successful in the first auditions and that there would be further auditions in London.

Watermelon

27 March 07

Five days later I was contacted by another *Big Brother* representative, and given details of auditions that were to take place at an unspecified location in London on 30th March. I asked him what to expect, and he told me that there would be an interview and some games. It was to last all day.

Big Brother would meet all my expenses as long as I kept the receipts. I was to take down with me my passport, bank card, two utility bills, police check evidence, doctor's details, details of my three most recent jobs, and the names and contact details of three friends and three relatives. I was also given details of how to make contact in London with the *Big*

Brother agent who would take me to the as yet unspecified location.

Until then the selection process had all been in the public domain, and had been advertised extensively to obtain the greatest response. However, now that *Big Brother* was dealing with those who had passed through the first stage, there was a need for secrecy, so as to prevent the press from disclosing who would or might be among the housemates. I have learned that reporters go to a lot of trouble trying to locate those who have been successful, even in the earlier rounds of the selection, and are willing to pay well for their stories. Those who are finally selected are whisked away by *Big Brother* to undisclosed locations across Britain and the Continent, and only allowed to reappear just before entering the *Big Brother* house.

Because of the danger of reporters telephoning and tricking me into admissions, I was told that I should not talk about *Big Brother* matters to anyone who had not first said the secret word 'Watermelon'. I should first ask, 'Have you anything to say to me?', and a genuine caller from *Big Brother* would say 'Watermelon'. Anyone who said 'Watermelon' could be trusted and I was to accept their instructions as genuine. I was told that I could disclose the code word to my wife Rukhsana, but that neither of us should disclose it to any other living soul.

A few weeks later, when secrecy was even more important, I came into the house and my little granddaughter Sara looked at me. I froze when she exclaimed: "Here comes the watermelon!" My first thought was that the cat was out of the bag. If Sara knew the secret then probably everyone did, and this was the end of game. But then I followed the direction of Sara's eyes and saw, yes, that I was carrying a big black watermelon for our tea!

Ms Lime-green

30 March 07

On the day of the London trip I took a taxi to Bradford station and caught an early train to King's Cross, remembering to obtain a receipt for the taxi fare. Arriving at King's Cross, I made my way by underground to Holborn, and went to the High Holborn & British Museum exit, where it had been arranged that I would make contact at 11.15am with a *Big Brother* agent, who would be carrying a lime-green umbrella with white spots.

I didn't leave the station, but stood still for a while at one side of the arched exit, letting the rush of other travellers go past. I searched around, waiting for a sight of the arrival of a lime-green umbrella, but couldn't see one anywhere. I had been given a mobile number to ring in case of emergencies, but I didn't want to have to use this. After a while I noticed through the rush of people that I was being regarded intently by an attractive young lady standing by the wall at the other side of the exit. I looked back, and our little head movements soon developed into nods. We swam towards each other through the crowd and I noticed the lime-green object in her hand, not as conspicuous as I had expected, by being folded up and out of the rain that was falling just a few feet away.

Once our identities had been established, Ms Lime-green turned out to be strictly business-like. I was led on a circuitous route around Holborn and taken through a side door of a large hotel being used by *Big Brother* for the day's auditions. Ms Lime-green took me to the *Big Brother* reception point, and left me with one of a number of other female agents. This one asked me for the documents I had taken down with me, and I obliged. She then gave me some notes for auditionees, which, when I read them a day or so later, I found to include warnings about the less pleasant consequences of appearing in the *Big Brother* program. These notes had been signed that day by P B Jones (Creative Director) on behalf of Brighter Pictures, the makers of *Big Brother*.

An extortionate taxi-fare

My new contact turned out to be acting as cashier, and, after she had examined and photocopied my passport, we came to the matter of my expenses. The train fare was high, in fact the maximum amount that British Rail could charge for the return journey at peak hours, but the cashier paid this sum without concern. However, when we came to the matter of the £4.70 taxi fare from my home to Bradford station, things became less straightforward, and confusion took over.

The confusion was brought about by the inadequacy of my taxi driver's knowledge of the decimal system. In fact he apparently did not think it to be necessary to insert a decimal point between the figure for pounds and that for the pence. The consequence was that unbeknown to me I had presented *Big Brother*'s cashier with a receipt for £470, for a fare that was actually £4.70!

She was startled when she saw what I had given her.

"Do you expect me to pay this!" she asked.

"Of course! Why not?" said I.

"We can't pay *this*!" she said.

"I'm afraid you'll have to," said I, becoming rather annoyed.

"No, no, impossible!" she said, becoming yet more annoyed herself, and she showed the receipt to another agent. I was beginning to wonder what sort of Big Brother was in charge of an organisation that would let the elephant pass through but not the tail!

"Look," I said, "Big Brother gave me his word on the phone that all expenses would be met. In fact you'll have to pay me as much again for going back!"

"You must be joking," she said. "Another four hundred and seventy pounds, just for a taxi?"

After this bolt from the blue I realised the truth, and put the cashier right. The situation, which until that point had been escalating to a dangerous level, suddenly resolved itself. The temperature went down, the taxi fare was met, and we became quite friendly again.

The secret room

I was then handed over to a guide, who took me to a secret room within the hotel, where I joined some more of the candidates of the day. This time we were given not one, but a whole set of questionnaires to fill in, and we were given the whole day to complete them. While the filling in was going on we were taken out individually for filmed auditions.

On being taken for my own audition I found myself before a panel of about ten persons. The chairman of the panel was conservatively dressed, and asked all the questions. The rest were very liberal in their appearance, and they just listened. I was determined not to treat the occasion like a job interview. I was being filmed, so I put some action into my responses and took the initiative where I could. After about a quarter-of-an-hour of this, I was returned to my questionnaires, which were waiting for me where I had left them.

Dreaded group activities

After we had all been individually taken off and given our filmed auditions, we left our questionnaires, and it was time for what I had been dreading – group activities. Even though I had been successful in Manchester, I was still apprehensive that I might not understand what was required. However, as at Manchester, I found that I did much better than I had feared – sometimes not just in spite of, but *because of* the fact that I really did misunderstand some of the main instructions!

It all went on for some two hours. There were three judges, one 'facilitator' who gave instructions, and a camerawoman with assistant. These officials, like the other candidates, were all much younger than me.

One of the judges halted the introductory proceedings to give us all a serious lecture. He told us that we should maintain complete secrecy about our day with *Big Brother*. This was to apply even if we were not selected, in that we might still be required at a later date, even after the program had started, as long as we had not talked to the press. He told us that one possible housemate replacement in a previous series had been passed over because he had earned himself a few hundred pounds by selling his story to a newspaper. (I later on discovered that *Big Brother* was asking on the website to be given any information anyone might have received about those who were to appear in the 2007 series!).

After the judge's lecture, the facilitator took up direction of activities again. He required, first of all, that we each give a short speech on one of a few given topics. I thought he added that we must speak 'without a breath', but I have since realised that what he really said must have been 'without a break'.

He asked for a volunteer and people started looking around for a victim. When some gazes rested on me, I decided to get the thing over and done with, and I went to the front, took a deep breath, and launched into a short but very quick dissertation on the subject of footballers' pay.

I spoke as fast as I could. It was something like: "Footballers shouldn't be paid colossal sums of money just for using their feet while I get paid so little for using my mind and my hands as well as my feet all day long it's bloody ludicrous preposterous ridiculous that they get paid so much only for kicking kicking a football but we'll all be equal in the end we'll all kick the bucket one day..." And, running out of breath, I had to stop.

One of the judges said there was still half a minute left, but I said I'd no breath left for any more. This must have sounded mysterious, but the judges let it go at that. I rejoined the group and was surprised at the warm welcome I received, like an old soldier finally returning from the battlefield to the hugs and kisses of his young comrades.

Later on we were asked to split up into two groups according to whether we were or weren't in favour of prisons. A debate was to take place between the two groups. I was in favour of prisons, but for some reason, which I cannot recall, I accidentally joined those who were against them. The result was that when I started arguing in favour of prisons I was preaching to the converted. The resulting confusion eventually resolved itself into laughter, and I had to make my way across to join my own kind.

One of the activities paralleled what actually takes place in the *Big Brother* house: we had to vote out one of our number. The victim of this exercise really did disappear, never to be seen again. But this surprised me as I thought we were merely acting. In fact, if I had been the victim I would have tried to come back into the room again to carry on where I had left off.

We were later asked to place everybody in the group in a line, honest at one end, dishonest at the other, according to our perceptions of them. When my turn came I found that I couldn't avoid hurting feelings. When I was asked to place myself among the rest, I chose the most honest position of all.

Finally some of us were asked to arrange the group according to perceived age. When my turn came, and I had finished arranging the others in a line, I didn't think to include myself in the arrangement. I stood next to the line I had just formed, and was surprised at the mirth this caused everyone. After a while, looking at the 18-year-old next to whom I was standing, I realised that I was supposed to be in the line as well, and I moved to the other end where I belonged.

Back to the questionnaires

When the activities concluded, we were taken back yet again to our questionnaires, and I continued with the endless questions, which I was determined to answer as well as I could. My determination must have been well above average, because I was eventually the only candidate left writing.

The questions were multiple choice, and most of them were designed to assess how candidates interact socially, whether they are followers or leaders, and to what extent they are creative thinkers.

One of the instructions was to leave a question alone if it made no sense. I did indeed find a question that made no sense, but I couldn't leave it alone. Instead I used my creativity, and my biro, to change it into a question that did make sense, and for which I had an answer.

In the end I suppose the staff wanted to turn the lights off and go home. One of the supervisors remarked that I oughtn't to take things so seriously. Eventually I was turned out of the building and told I could finish the questionnaire when I came back. I rushed to King's Cross and caught a late train to Bradford.

I flopped down in my seat, happy with the recollection of the words 'you can finish it when you come back' and the thought that I had apparently done well enough to be asked to continue to a further stage.

Forced to act

My elation was soon disturbed when I remembered what the judge had said in his lecture, that we should tell no one about what we were doing. One consequence of this was that I would be unable to share my elation with my children, who had prompted me to start on the whole process, who knew where I had come that day, and who would be eagerly waiting to hear what had happened.

I was distressed at the thought of having to deceive them, but there was no alternative. My children had many friends whom they trusted, and those friends had trusted friends, and so on *ad infinitum*. The problem was how I could possibly prevent myself from telling them the truth: that I felt certain I had done very well. With a heavy heart, I realised I had to pretend I had failed. But I could not think how to do this, until I recalled the eviction exercise of the afternoon. I decided to use the experience of the victim as the basis for the script I now put together in my mind to help me when I arrived home.

Rukhsana was with the others as I walked in. There was therefore no opportunity to speak to her by herself before I had to make a statement to the family. When I had returned from

Manchester my feelings had been as clear on my face as the *Big Brother* stamp on my hand. This time, however, I hung my head, and was silent. They realised something must be wrong.

Eventually, Rushda asked, "What happened?"

I shook my head. "I couldn't do it... it was too much for me..." And then I recounted, as my own, the experience of the only man to be eliminated from the proceedings.

After this there was a three minute silence. But then Rushda comforted me: "Oh well, never mind Dad. These things happen." And she told me to remember how well I had done to get as far as I had.

The family dispersed, and left me with my unhappiness at what I had been obliged to do – unhappiness, but not guilt. For, as I saw it, my children would benefit in the end. At the first opportunity, I told Rukhsana what had really happened, and included an account of the lecture on secrecy. Her face lit up again. She agreed that I had acted for the best. We both looked forward to the time when we would be able to tell the children the truth. If I did succeed in getting on the program, the disclosure would be a joyous occasion indeed!

Questioning my sanity

31 March 07

The next contact from *Big Brother* was much sooner than I expected. On Saturday morning, the next day, the telephone rang. When I answered, the caller said nothing to my repeated Hello's. Then, after a long pause, I said, "Have you anything to say to me?" And this elicited a response. "Watermelon," said a voice that I recognised. "Well done! Congratulations!"

I had survived the previous day's ordeal! But this was not the end. Before I could be whisked away to the protective surroundings of a continental hotel, I first had to survive one further trial. I was required to go to London again on Tuesday 3rd April for psychological tests that would take place on the 4th. In other words, they wanted to find out if I was sane! There were to be two interviews on the Wednesday: one in the morning and one in the afternoon.

The reader might by now not be surprised to learn that I failed on this final day. But, at the time, I was experiencing no doubts about my own sanity – though I was certainly having doubts about Big Brother's.

2 April 07

You might say that my doubts about Big Brother were confirmed when I was contacted again on Monday and told that a hotel booking had been made for me in the name of Mahmud *Chhokar*, at the Ambassadors in Bloomsbury, for the following night!

I was instructed that, at 9am, on the morning of Wednesday the 4th, I was to be at the McDonald's on Platform 2 of Victoria Train Station, to meet a man with an umbrella (colour unspecified!) who would take me to the first interview. In the afternoon I was to stand outside Pret A Manger at 92 Buckingham Palace Road at 1.30pm, to be contacted by yet another agent, who would take me to the second interview.

Jokers at the Ambassadors

3 April 07

Tuesday came, and I had again been obliged to lie to my children, telling them that I was going on business to Birmingham, and might have to stay overnight. Instead, I went to London again, and to the Ambassadors hotel. At check-in I said I was Mr Chhokar, and sure enough a booking had been made under that name.

A problem arose straight away, as *Big Brother* had only paid for Chhokar's bed and breakfast. If I wanted anything else I would have to hand over my credit card to the clerk. I had almost done this when I remembered that my real name was on the card. I realised that, if I handed it over, my cover would be blown. I couldn't think of any good reason to refuse, and the clerk was insistent that unless I handed it over I would be unable to use any of the hotel's services. In the end I saw my way out of the difficulty and deposited £20 for services, and the sweat on my forehead started to disappear.

It was vital that on the following morning I should wake up in time for my Victoria contact, otherwise I would have wasted all the successful effort I had so far put in. I arranged with the desk to give me a wake-up call at 7am, but I was not sure that I could rely on this. I rang Rukhsana and told her that I had arrived, and I asked her, just in case, to ring me in the morning if I didn't ring her by 7am. Rukhsana and I had rarely been apart, and she rang me again that evening, about midnight, to say goodnight.

It was then that the machinations of *Big Brother* rebounded on Rukhsana as well as on me. When she asked to be put through to me, she accidentally mispronounced my assumed name and asked for 'Mr Joker'! The desk asked her who was calling, and she was able to say with confidence (because it was true) that she was his wife. Then came the difficulty. The receptionist asked Rukhsana to spell the name. Rukhsana now found herself in the embarrassing position of not being able to spell 'Chhokar' – that is, her husband's and her own name!

The seconds ticked by, and the only way out of this dilemma seemed to be to hang up. Fortunately, however, I had told Rukhsana my room number, and she had the presence of mind to ask just to be put through to room 315. The crisis over, she was soon talking to me, and before we finished I reminded her that she was to call me in the morning. She advised me to go straight to bed, and not long afterwards I did so, and soon fell into a deep sleep.

4 April 07

I was shaken out of my blissful state by an excruciating ringing sound in my ears and I was out of bed in seconds. In my confusion, I did not think about what might have been the origin of the ringing, which had now stopped, and I immediately phoned my wife.

"Rukhsana, I'm up," I said. "No need to ring me!"

"Are you mad?" she exclaimed. "It's only three o' clock!"

I thought she was mistaken, but I looked at my watch, and sure enough it agreed with what I had been told. Our conversation didn't go on much after that, and I was soon in bed again. However, it took me some while to get back to sleep, and I lay there wondering what sort of big brother I was dealing with, who could put me through such horrendous experiences.

I was woken by Rukhsana at 6.50am. Ten minutes later, I heard the phone ringing again while I was still in the shower, but I just let it ring until it stopped.

I got myself ready, went downstairs, had breakfast, and went straight to the desk to check out. As I was about to leave the hotel, the receptionist asked whether I had received my requested wake-up call. Being reminded of the ringing in the early morning, I replied that it had been a little earlier than expected. "Sorry Sir," she said, "but I think that one was the fire-alarm!"

Mr Black Umbrella

At 9am I was standing outside McDonald's on Platform 2, Victoria Train Station, looking for an umbrella. But the *Big Brother* agent was not yet in position. As a result I spent the next 5 minutes feeling rather foolish. Although it was not raining, some of the people coming towards me were carrying umbrellas. Two or three times I moved forward to meet what I took to be *Big Brother*'s man, only for him to sweep by on his way.

After I had given up this useless pursuit, the genuine article came from the opposite direction, having just alighted from his train. His umbrella was black. He made himself known to me, phoned headquarters to say he had made contact, and then escorted me to the morning's venue, a nearby hotel.

On this occasion I saw no other candidates, and as far as I could tell only a few of the hotel's rooms had been taken by *Big Brother*. First of all, Mr Black Umbrella took me to a guest room, one which appeared well lived-in, and he paid me my expenses so far, without any problems this time. He then handed me the questionnaire from last time to finish, and three psychological multiple choice test papers to resolve the question of my sanity!

While I was busy at my work, Mr Black Umbrella must have slipped away, for I never saw him again. In his place appeared a young man who said that he had been involved in the Manchester auditions, and had been one of the facilitators.

Uncalled-for help

I finished the previous questionnaire, and then set to work to prove my sanity. The first of the three written psychological tests seemed straightforward enough and apparently designed to identify me as a follower or as a leader again. The second test had an added requirement in that it was timed, but I managed to complete it, and this took me to the third test.

At this point the *modus operandi* mysteriously changed, and the facilitator-turned-invigilator took the test paper from me, and read out the questions. As I replied, he wrote *Yes* or *No* or ticked the appropriate boxes on my behalf, or, in the case of the final question, wrote a few words. If I didn't properly hear any question, he would repeat it, and sometimes rephrase it, to make it more comprehensible. When he was filling in my answers he would sometimes have to think about the questions himself, and he would indicate that my answer was correct. When he said that if he got any answers wrong his boss would sack him, he was clearly not joking, and it began to seem to me as though I had already been selected!

It was with the final question that I had real trouble. I cannot remember what it was, except that its grammatical structure seemed to be outside of my range. Because I was obliged to answer, I made a guess, and was told that my answer was wrong, and the question was read out again. I made another guess, and this was wrong as well. I asked to read the question myself, but even reading it didn't help, and my third attempted answer was, like the others, judged to be unsatisfactory. The facilitator-turned-invigilator then took the test paper back and completed it for me in a way that seemed to please him well enough. He must have been the world's most helpful invigilator – at least I hope so, for I never actually saw any of my own answers!

The *modus operandi* adopted with the final test is very mysterious indeed. It is not credible that the invigilator would write down my responses on his own authority. A number of conspiracy theories have crossed my mind since then, but the most likely explanation seems to be that it had already been decided that I would be in the program.

It has since become clear to me that the psychological tests were not a part of the original selection process for *Big Brother* in the year 2000, but were a later addition. It may be that they were designed only in the interests of the housemates, and are perhaps not welcomed by all the selectors. They might even have been imposed because of legal considerations arising out of a duty of care that the program has towards those who take part in it.

The psychologist

The invigilator now took me along for the first of my two interviews of the day. The morning interview was to be with a psychologist, and I would see a psychiatrist in the afternoon.

On the way to this first interview, we talked about the live launch of the program, when all the housemates would come out of hiding and be shown to the public for the first time. The invigilator told me that he would be personally responsible for taking my wife to London, for taking her to her hotel, for escorting her to the launch, and for arranging her return to

Bradford. While I was in the *Big Brother* house my wife would be able to ring a special number if there were any problems. They would be constantly in touch with her, and provide all the help and support she needed. And they would arrange for her return to London if they suspected that, under the rules of the show, I was going to be voted out of the *Big Brother* house.

This kind of talk certainly confirmed me in my thought that I was to be in the program, and my daydreams about the pleasant consequences of becoming a celebrity seemed close enough to be real. Not only would the future of *The Logic of Half a Moustache* be assured, but there would be many sources of income arising out of my experience. There would be payments for newspaper articles, television and radio appearances, and maybe even a permanent engagement. Maybe I'd even start an acting career and meet Shilpa Shetty – who, the invigilator told me, had recently been given an advertising contract with Marks & Spencer. The possibilities seemed endless. Everything had gone right so far and I just had two further hurdles to jump: the psychologist now and the psychiatrist in the afternoon.

The first interview lasted an hour. It was conducted in a formal manner, and although dealing with many matters, it was aimed principally at finding out how well I would cope with 3 months locked up in the *Big Brother* house. I laughed and said that I could manage for several years! I also said that I understood that if accepted for the program I would become 'public property' (an expression used in the *Big Brother* literature). Asked about the possibility of not getting in, I said that this would not matter much, and that I would continue with my writing projects. At the end of the interview the psychologist said, "I see no problem!" We shook hands and I left.

In limbo

I now had a long break before the next interview, which was to be at 3 o'clock instead of the 1.30pm originally arranged. I phoned Rukhsana to tell her about what I took to have been a successful morning. I then found out how to reach Buckingham Palace Road and walked there at a leisurely pace. Arriving at Pret A Manger too early for my rendezvous, I went inside for something to eat, and stayed for over half an hour. I came out again and waited on the pavement for about 5 minutes until 3 o'clock.

I had been given no clues to help me identify the *Big Brother* agent who was to contact me, and I had to rely on the agent finding me. At the appointed time, a lady crossing the road from the other side smiled and seemed to be waving at me. I took a chance, waved back, and walked towards her. She retreated to the far side again, and when I reached her we greeted each other and it was apparent that she was indeed the agent sent to contact me.

She then took me on a 10 minute walk to the next venue, a large building, the front of which I never saw. We went through a rear entrance, by lift to an upper floor, and into a small room containing two chairs and a bed. One of the chairs was occupied by a young man, the reason for whose presence, to start with, was less than clear. I sat on the other chair, and the female agent sat down next to us on the edge of the bed.

No one said anything for a while. Then I asked the young man, a teenager, why he was there, and he said that he was waiting for someone. I talked to him, and as I did so I soon began to suspect that he was there to test my willingness or ability to converse with the young. But this didn't disturb me at all. In fact I talked to him for about 20 minutes, during which time he made very little contribution, other than to respond briefly to my occasional questions.

Meanwhile, the female agent kept her head down, pretending not to be there. She didn't actually take notes, but I'm sure she was listening carefully. When I spoke directly to her, she was startled, lifted her head for a moment and smiled, but said nothing. I had probably gone outside the parameters of the sociological test she was conducting.

The young man's involvement was put beyond doubt when he, together with the female agent, took me along to the psychiatrist's office for my final interview.

The Talk of Doom

When I went into the psychiatrist's office, he invited me to sit opposite him, and I found that he was smoking heavily. During the early part of our talk, he took quick puffs from his cigarette and blew these across his desk at me. I could only bear this for about two minutes before I said that it was too stuffy for me, and would he mind opening the window. After opening the window, he stubbed his cigarette out in the ash tray on his desk. All this was presumably a test to see whether I had spoken truly when I had written in the Manchester questionnaire that I am concerned about healthy living and the dangers of passive smoking.

Unlike the morning interview with the psychologist, the one with the psychiatrist was very informal, and it lasted perhaps twice as long. I was encouraged to talk about all aspects of my life, and he asked questions and took notes as I spoke. Later in the interview he gave me what I have come to realise was the 'Talk of Doom', referred to on the *Big Brother* website. He went deeply into some of the warnings given in the notes for auditionees of 30th March that I had been given on my previous London visit, and he asked if I had thought carefully about the pros and cons of becoming a celebrity.

My whole life, he said, would be irreversibly changed. I would have to give up my present reclusive kind of existence and would become 'public property'. While this had not fazed me before, I became more doubtful when he explained that this would also apply to my wife and children. Even a simple thing like going shopping would become hazardous – not just because of the press, or fans wanting autographs, but also because there might be unpleasant people who would hurl abuse at me and my family. My reaction at the time was to say that I appreciated what he said but that I still wanted to go ahead. He asked me to think hard about it all the same, and to discuss it seriously with my wife. The assumption seemed to be that I would be contacted to see if I still felt happy about appearing in the program.

The way that I felt, while listening to the Talk of Doom, was rather like a lottery winner might feel if, after being given the cheque, he is given advice about the hazards of great wealth. He feels only the elation of his success, and any dangers are incidental or unimportant; and he certainly has no thought that, if he doesn't properly appreciate the dangers, the cheque will be cancelled!

The interview had been friendly, and I was full of confidence. The psychiatrist opened his fridge and pressed a chilled bottle of mineral water into my hand for my journey back to Bradford. Then he took me to the lift and we said our farewells.

The End

I went to King's Cross station, and before catching the train back to Bradford, I telephoned Rukhsana to tell her that all had gone extremely well, and that I would certainly be on the program. The journey back to Bradford was spent daydreaming about the exciting times ahead of me, both in the *Big Brother* house and afterwards in the transformed life that was to come.

These dreams lasted for a few days, but they faded as more and more time went by without anyone contacting me again from *Big Brother*, not even to tell me that I had been eliminated.

I watched the launch of the new *Big Brother* series on 30th May 2007, but I saw no one I recognised from my experience of the selection process. I knew from the judge's lecture of 30th

March that new housemates could be called even during the series. So it wasn't until the end of the series that I knew for certain that my lottery cheque had been cancelled, and that if my life was going to be transformed it would not be as a result of appearing in *Big Brother*.

However, my increased understanding of the nature of the program, and of the consequences of appearing in it, have since brought me to the realisation that, by not selecting me, Big Brother may well have done me a great service – that, whether intentionally or not, he has indeed acted as my big brother.

Executive Producer of *Big Brother*'s Interview interviewed for *Big Brother* website

What kinds of tests are done to ensure the housemates are suitable to go in the house?

We have a series of very thorough checks that all potential housemates have before we will even consider offering them a place in the *Big Brother* house. All of our potential housemates are also given something that we call the 'Talk of Doom', where we actively encourage them to think carefully about the impact that taking part in *Big Brother* could have on their lives.

It's important that, in addition to us assessing whether someone is right for the *Big Brother* house, each potential housemate thinks about whether *Big Brother* is right for him or her.

The Child's World

The Child's World

Children are fantastic. I didn't know what I was missing, until I had my own children: Mahboob, Rukhshanda and Rushda, followed by my grandchildren Sara and Rehan.

Being new arrivals in this world, children give us new ways of looking at what might well have become commonplace for us. For me, playing with the children, watching them, and listening to them, has been a rich source not only of fun and humour but also of science – indeed, if we let them, children can prompt us to reflect on questions which are really very profound.

Magic Jantrees

When I was a small boy, I lived in Pakistan. I was playing outside my house with a few friends one day when a vendor attracted our attention. He was selling what he called 'Magic Jantrees'. *Jantrees* were tiny booklets containing all sorts of weird things, ranging from treatments for illnesses to (what were said to be) efficacious prayers for health, wealth, success, and so forth.

The vendor told us that if anybody fainted in the hot midday sun, one of his Jantrees could be used to bring him to his senses. The Jantree had to be moved round and round over the person's head seven times and, lo and behold, he would recover! He then made a request: “If I faint in this heat, will someone please take a Jantree out of my shirt pocket and move it round seven times over my head, as I have just shown you. This would be a great kindness to me, and I would be much obliged.”

While he was telling us other things about his Jantrees, he suddenly staggered, fumbled, fainted, and fell down. We began to panic seeing the man lying prostrate before us on the ground. However, no one had the courage to take one of the Jantrees out of the man’s pocket. We just stood there, trembling, and looking at the man without doing anything.

The sun continued to beat down on him. After quite a while, we noticed some small eye movements: sometimes one eye opened slightly and sometimes the other. This only frightened us more.

Eventually, we noticed some movement in one of his hands, which then started crawling towards his shirt pocket. Slowly he retrieved one of his Jantrees, and started moving it round and round just above his head. We were transfixed. After the seventh circuit, he suddenly opened his eyes and jumped up, completely revived. We were all of us so impressed with the vendor’s Jantrees that he was sold out in no time.

Windy trees

I was taking my 4 year old granddaughter Sara for a walk in the park one day, when a strong wind started to blow.

“Sara, where do you think the wind comes from?” I asked.

After some thought, she looked at the trees, bending in the wind, and said, “The trees make it when they shake.”

“That’s a very good theory,” I said. “And look! That one’s shaken so hard it’s fallen over!”

“Poor tree,” she said.

A dental inspection

Sara climbed onto my lap one day and started to check my teeth individually. She was soon counting them for me.

"One, two, three, five, six..."

"Why did you miss number four?" I interrupted her.

"Look, Granddad," she pointed. "You've got a tooth missing, just here."

Copycat

When Sara was trying to draw a cat, I helped her by holding her hand and guiding it. Later on I again saw her attempting to draw a cat. This time she was holding her own hand and trying to guide it!

Sara then asked my friend Richard to draw a cat for her, while she was sitting opposite him at a table. When he was finished, Sara turned round to me and said, "Granddad, Granddad, Richard's really clever! He can draw a cat upside down!"

Close friends

I heard Sara talking to her friend Samantha on the phone:

"Look at my new shoes! The colour's nice, isn't it?"

What children want

Infants and young children display bizarre choices and have their own way of understanding the world. They cannot be relied upon to like what we like for them.

As a toddler, my granddaughter Sara was quite consistent in this matter. When we gave her a tiny tricycle, she was more interested in turning it upside down and playing with the wheels than in being pushed along on it. When we peeled an orange for her, she was more interested in the peel, and started gobbling it up, taking no notice of the soft juicy reward inside.

Are young children foolishly missing out on what's good for them, or are they seeing value where we have come to be blind to it?

A child's confidence is in your hands

First of all, show a child a marble in one of your hands. Put both hands behind your back and close them, one of them containing the marble. Bring your closed fists forward and ask the child which one contains the marble.

After a few games of this, secretly slip a marble into the other hand as well. Now you have two marbles, one in each fist. But the child thinks you have exactly one. Every time the child chooses a hand, they win!

The opposite game would be to secretly drop the only marble into your pocket. Now your hands are empty, but the child thinks you have exactly one marble. Every time the child chooses a hand, they lose!

Which of these two games you prefer might tell you more about yourself than the child.

A woodlouse's dilemma

"Granddad, look!" Sara exclaimed. "What a big woodlouse!"

On looking, I discovered that it was a mouse. What should the mouse make of Sara's mistake, in terms of its self-esteem?

Toying with words

"Mummy, my nose is having a cold," a young child told her mother. "That's why my eyes couldn't sleep last night!"

When children begin to pick up language, they often use it in strange and unconventional ways. In the early stages, words can be completely mismatched with concepts, producing amusing results.

I once overheard my granddaughter Sara say to her friend, "We are wearing the *same* colours: you are wearing blue, and I am *also* wearing red!" I wonder where the tangle occurred?

On a separate occasion, Sara saw two people, and I overheard her say ponderously to my son Mahboob, "Dad, they look just like each other. They must be neighbours."

Is it a bird?

When Sara was only 10 months old, any bird in the sky was a pigeon, as far as she was concerned.

Once she pointed towards the sky and started shouting with delight: "Pigeon! Pigeon! Pigeon!" I looked up, and it was a helicopter.

Is it a plane?

"Daddy, what is that thing over there in the sky?" my tiny daughter Rushda asked me when she was very young.

"That's an aeroplane; it carries people," I replied.

Rushda considered the response for a moment.

"But it's such a tiny thing. How do the people squeeze in?" she queried.

"It's a special plane for tiny people," I couldn't resist.

Sweetening the deal

Once, a father said to his 5 year old son, "Pohlu, if I have one sweet for you in one hand and two in the other, tell me how many I've got for you altogether."

Pohlu's eyes lit up, and his mouth watered. He began desperately calculating the answer to the conundrum. The father looked pleased that he'd succeeded in getting Pohlu to do some arithmetic.

"No, Pohlu!" cried his older sister suddenly. "Don't answer. It's a trick! Daddy hasn't really got any sweets for you. He's just trying to get you to do some maths!" She'd clearly been through it all herself.

Pohlu turned away and the problem remained unsolved.

Child genius?

Once, a friend of mine thought his son was quite clever in arithmetic. To put this to the test, I asked his son, "If with one pound you could buy two apples, how many would you be able to buy with two pounds?"

"Four," he replied.

Then I asked, "If in one hour you could walk two miles, how many miles could you walk in two hours?"

"Four," he answered.

Finally I asked, "If with one eye you could see two marbles, how many would you see with two eyes?"

"Four, of course!" he replied promptly, beginning to sound annoyed.

Lucky pigeon!

We were once crossing the road with Sara. Naturally, her mum insisted on holding her hand throughout, though on this occasion, Sara yearned for independence.

"Why can't I cross the road by myself, Mum?" Sara objected. "Look at that little pigeon. *He's* crossing by himself!"

Hide and seek

"I have hidden something for you to find," said my son Mahboob one day, when he was a small boy.

"Where have you hidden it?" I asked.

"I'm not saying."

"Okay, at least tell me *what* you've hidden."

"I'm not going to tell you that either."

I like a good challenge.

A cautious ball

Sara and I were playing with a ball in our hall one evening. During the game, the ball bounced into the lounge, where my wife Rukhsana was watching television, and when Sara had retrieved it she shut the door behind her to stop the ball going in anymore.

Later on, when Rukhsana came out of the lounge, she turned off the light and left the door open. I expected Sara to close the door again, but she continued with the game, quite unconcerned.

I asked her, "Aren't you going to close the door, in case the ball goes in?"

"Oh, it won't go in there now," she replied wisely. "It's too dark."

Beating the weather

One Sunday, little Rushda reminded me to buy some chocolate for her the next day, when I would be going to the superstore. I said that the weather forecast was that it might rain on Monday, either in the morning or in the afternoon. So I couldn't promise.

Rushda had a solution. "If it rains in the morning, go in the afternoon. And if it rains in the afternoon, go in the morning. Simple!"

Father, me and the paratha

When I was little, Chacha, my father, took me to a local primary school in Rawalpindi where he wanted me to be admitted. We made our way to an open-air class which was in progress. The teacher sat on a chair at the front, while the children sat on the ground, or on mats, or piles of bricks.

Chacha explained the purpose of our visit, and the teacher gave me a test to see if I was suitable for admission – a long division sum. I immediately took my slate from my satchel and set to work. Chacha, who was completely illiterate, looked on, not understanding what I was doing. For him it appeared that all was going well. But at the end, the teacher looked at my answer, and shook his head with disappointment. I had flunked my entry exam!

We walked all the way home without exchanging a word. On the way, I became more and more frightened as to what would happen when we arrived, and Mother, who would be anxiously waiting, heard of my failure. I knew that other children were punished extremely severely in similar situations.

When we arrived back, before Mother could say a word, Chacha said to her: "First of all, make something for my son to eat. He has worked very hard at his test, and he is in need of sustenance."

Happily anticipating good news, Mother immediately took some dough and started to make a *paratha*, one of her special treats, made with extra *ghee*. When it was ready, golden and juicy, and very hot, Mother started to ask about our visit to the school, but Chacha said, "There's no rush. Let him finish first. Then we'll tell you everything."

I relished the delicious paratha and took my time. When I had finished, Chacha gave me a glass of water, and turned to Mother, who was becoming desperate for the news. Chacha said, "I'm afraid he failed."

The following week, Chacha took me along to another school, where I was given a place. When we arrived home again, Chacha straight away told Mother the good news that I had been admitted.

"I knew it. I knew he could do it this time," said Mother, reaching for the paratha dough once more.

"Oh, it was easy enough," said Chacha. "There wasn't a test this time."

I had plain *daal* for dinner as usual.

Playing by the rules

Many parents, while valuing education, fail to appreciate the educational value of pure play. To their minds, play by itself is quite useless.

But knowing that their children love to play, these parents become easy prey to the thought that their children can be tricked into learning while they play. To start with, this leads the parents to adopt the compromise, as they see it, of the *educational toy*. But as the years go by, they lose all conception of what a toy really is, and they concentrate entirely on the educational element.

There are parents who firmly believe that a ruler is a toy. I recently heard of a boy who found in his Christmas stocking: a book about mental arithmetic, a ruler, three pencils, a sharpener and several sheets of graph paper!

Sara's cure

I was once playing with Sara and her various toy animals. We were having great fun experimenting with different scenarios for the creatures, when Sara made an innovative suggestion:

"Let's kill the mouse," she said excitedly.

Seizing the moment to encourage her to become more morally aware, I said, "But Sara, if we killed the mouse, its baby would be really sad!"

"Don't worry Granddad," Sara comforted me. "We could kill the baby too."

The benefits of dreams

"Daddy, you promised me you'd get me some new toys," my young daughter Rukhshanda reminded me one day, when she was very young.

"When was that?" I asked.

"It was in a dream I had last night."

"I can't remember what I said in your dream!" I objected.

"Well, you *did* say it," she insisted. "You can ask Rushda, if you don't believe me. She was with us when you promised."

A childish pact

Two children, best friends, were beginning to be quite health conscious. One day, they made the following pact to encourage themselves:

"We'll never smoke, even when we grow up. Promise?"

"Promise!"

"If you do, I won't speak to you again."

"And if *you* do, I won't speak to *you*."

"Okay. And if we *both* smoke, we won't speak to each other again – promise?"

"Promise!"

Does God smoke?

"Dad, is God a boy or a girl?" Rukhshanda once asked me.

"Neither!" I said.

"Does God smoke?" she asked again.

"Nope!" I replied.

"How do you know?" she asked me sceptically.

Unexpected response?

"Can you hear me, Sara?"

"No."

Drinking up

I once saw my granddaughter Sara drinking some juice on her own. I was impressed when, without prior demonstration, she tilted her head and glass right back so as to drink the last of the juice. Later, I was even more impressed when, without prompting, I saw her sucking juice from a glass through a drinking straw.

On a still later occasion, she had finished what she could from a glass of juice, with the straw dangling in its original position. I expected her to lower the straw in the glass. Instead, to get at what remained, she suddenly tilted the glass and her head right back, with the straw still in her mouth!

This attempt to apply the standard technique to a non-standard situation resulted in Sara's drink being deposited outside her body rather than inside it. I was not impressed at all.

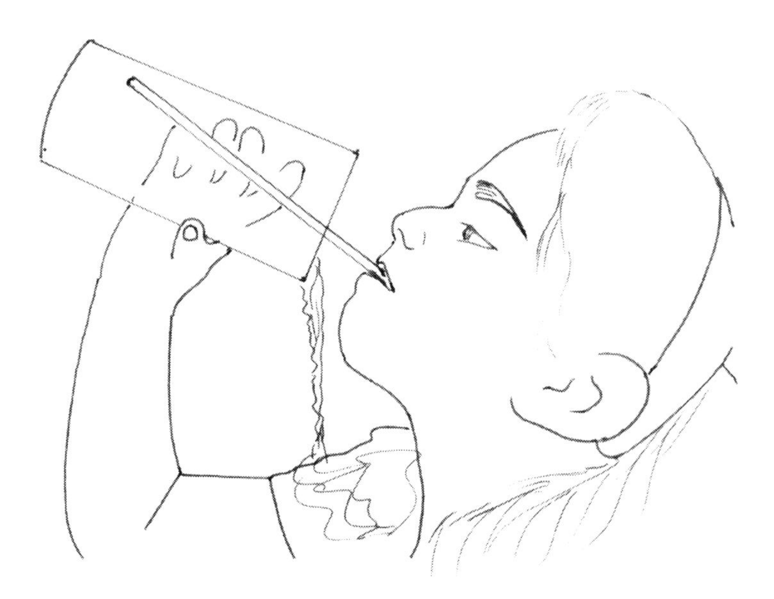

Reality check

One day, when little Rukhshanda was very happy with some new toys, I said to her, "You never know, you might only be dreaming that you have got some new toys!"

She puzzled over this for a while, and presently replied, "No, I am not dreaming, Daddy. Come on, let's go and see."

She took me into her bedroom, and pointed to the bed.

"There, you see! The bed's empty. So I can't be dreaming!"

If babies could talk

As with other infants, my little grandson Rehan's early days were largely spent trying to put everything within reach into his mouth.

I was wondering about this one day, and said to his Mum, "If only Rehan could talk, I'd be able to ask him why he does it."

His Mum gave me what I regard as a true insight: "If he could talk, all he'd say would be, 'I can't help it'."

Keeping toys under wraps

When giving presents to children, parents always impose some degree of discipline to ensure careful and proper handling; and if a toy is meant to be educational, parents make a particular effort to prevent any funny business. Children are often reprimanded if they misuse their presents: a plastic telephone as a hammer, or a dolly as a football.

On the other hand, children are unrestricted in the ways they can play with the wrappings, and this loosening of the reins makes the wrappings much more enjoyable. For very young children, the wrappings are the real presents, and the items inside are only there to hold the wrappings in place!

Wrappings allow children more freedom as to what they might do with them, and they offer numerous possibilities of innovation and experimentation. Because of the discipline attached to the presents, children can never be said to fully 'own' their gifts. But the wrapping paper is theirs in the truest sense!

Parents who properly understand the educational uses of wrapping paper will not be bothered about the degree of disorder that might develop in the living room when a child ravages a present. Indeed, they will welcome it as a sign that things are going well. Mess is good.

Indeed, parents should consider using educational wrapping paper instead of educational toys. It wouldn't matter anymore what was contained in the parcel. Any old object would do – a scarf, say, or a plastic cup, even some more wrapping paper, or just nothing at all. All the interest and the value of the gift would reside in the paper.

How to lose a child's custom

Once when we were in town, we gave Rukhshanda a £5 note to buy whatever she wanted. Browsing through a shop, she saw a video she liked, priced at £4.99.

"I've only got five pounds," Rukhshanda said dismally. "I'll have to save up until I have enough!"

Considerate pool staff

Sara has always enjoyed going to the swimming pool with her Mum. She was talking about it excitedly one day, when I asked her directly, "Sara, are you sure you can swim yet?"

Her response was prompt: "Of course – with arm-bands!"

On a later occasion I went to the swimming pool with them. Halfway through, just after re-entering the pool, Sara turned to me and exclaimed, "Granddad, when I come out of the water and jump back in again, they make it warmer for me."

The wrong trousers

Joe, the youngest son of one of my friends, used to wear his older brother Sam's clothes when Sam had outgrown them.

One day when we were all looking through my friend's family photographs, we came across one of Sam, taken at a time before Joe's birth. On seeing this photograph, Joe exclaimed: "Look! Sam is wearing *my* trousers!"

A difficult question

"Where did I come from, Daddy?" my daughter Rukhshanda once asked me when she was little.

I confidently answered this difficult question as you might expect. "You came from your Mummy's tummy," I said.

"Then why do I look like *you*? That's what Aunty says," she queried. This was a much more difficult question to answer! I changed the subject.

What a silly question!

I once told off a little boy in our street:

"You annoy everyone who passes by. You break milk bottles on the footpath. You tip over our dustbins. You're a nuisance! What is the matter with you? *Why don't you behave yourself?*"

"'Cos I'm a naughty boy!" he replied with pride.

Plastic wasps

Sara once said, "Granddad, I am scared of wasps. They bite!" Having previously seen plastic toys shaped like animals and bugs, she continued, "Can I have some plastic wasps to get used to? Then the real ones won't scare me."

A winter illusion

The first time Sara saw a hill completely blanketed with snow, she was astounded. With a sweeping wave of her arm, she gestured at the entire hill, and cried, "Look at that great big heap of snow!"

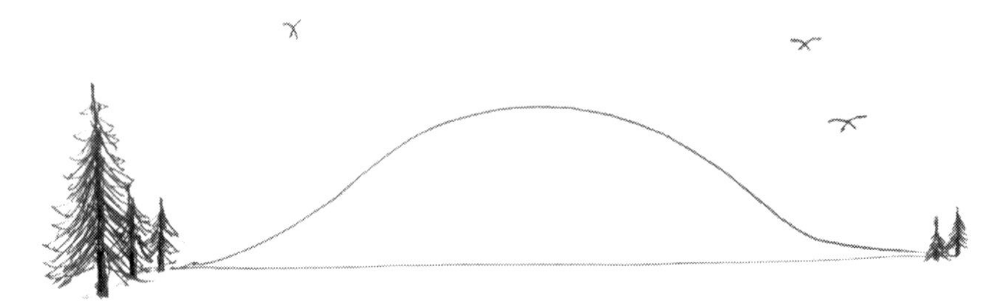

Lights out

Rukhshanda panicked and screamed one evening when suddenly everything went pitch black. She was playing on the computer, and this was her first experience of a power-cut.

We all came rushing and I explained there was no need to panic. Sure enough, in a couple of minutes' time the power was restored and the lights came on again.

Rukhshanda breathed a sigh of relief. "I thought I had gone blind!"

Light and dark

I have always been intrigued by the workings of the Universe, and have wanted to inspire a similar curiosity in my children and grandchildren.

Once, hoping to teach a little science, I asked Sara, "Sara, why can't we see the Sun at night?"

She looked at me as though I had asked a pointless question, and answered, "Because it's too dark!"

A technical victory

Sara loves to do jigsaws. She loves it even more when someone else does it with her. However, she loves it best when she competes with them, each doing their own jigsaw.

Once, Sara and my wife Rukhsana decided to have a jigsaw competition. They each had a jigsaw, and the first to finish would be the winner. Unfortunately for Sara, on this occasion, Rukhsana was taking it all much too seriously, and was determined to win.

After a few minutes, Sara wasn't making a lot of progress, but Rukhsana was just about to finish. Sara was growing desperate.

At the last moment, just as Rukhsana was reaching for her last piece, Sara snatched it up and quickly put it into place, finishing Rukhsana's jigsaw.

"Yes! I'm the winner!" she shouted.

Rectification of a mistake

Once, when I was bringing some things in from the garden, Sara stopped me and said, "Granddad, bring my shoes in as well."

"But you're wearing them!" I reminded her.

"Sorry, Granddad!" she said. She took off a shoe and flung it into the garden, then did the same with the other. Having rectified her mistake, she said, "*Now* bring them in!"

An easier way to exercise

I like to jog three times round the park, and I do so regularly. One day, when I came home puffing from my exercise, Sara asked me if jogging was difficult. I told her that the first lap was always easy but that the third one was very hard.

Sara pondered for some time. Later on, she came back to me beaming, with a solution. "Granddad, why don't you do the third lap first?"

Mummy Owl and the Three Baby Owls

One day Sara asked me to read her the story of *Mummy Owl and the Three Baby Owls*. Rukhsana had already read her the story a few times, but this was my first reading.

After a while, the situation with the three baby owls was becoming very tense, as they waited for Mummy Owl to return. I stopped reading for a while to express my concern.

"I'm getting really worried," I said. "What's going to happen if Mummy Owl doesn't come back? The babies won't have anything to eat!"

Sara looked into my worried face and whispered, "Don't worry Granddad, Mummy Owl comes back on page five."

Reciprocating

When I picked up Sara from the nursery one day, she told me about her new friend Amina. "If I like something, she gives it to me. If I don't like something, I give it to her."

Play

Children love to play, and they will play with anyone who is willing. They play with their friends, and they play best with their best friends. Becoming a parent is an opportunity to regain the love of play you had when you were young. And joining in with your children is an opportunity to become more than just their parent, but their friend, and maybe even their best friend.

Why do children play? As far as they're concerned, they play because they like it. But why do they like it?

Humans are not the only species whose young engage in play. And when we see the play of animals, we can start to understand that it is a necessary preparation for adulthood. Can we not see the play of human children in the same light?

In fact, when viewed in this way, play is to be seen as a form of education. If a child were never to play, the resulting adult would not be able to relate successfully with the world of adults. And not only would a child lose the educational value of play, but also the pure fun of the play itself.

What is real education? We come into this world with five senses, like tentacles with which we contact, understand and make sense of the world and ourselves. All our theories, conjectures and observations derive from our senses, and are ultimately tested by the senses for acceptance or rejection. Our senses are the arbiters. But we also learn, through our senses, that our senses can themselves be fallible! So we also need to learn when and when not to trust our senses. In this case, the intellect is the final arbiter.

Real education, I believe, is nothing other than the sharpening both of our senses and of our intellect. And play, which certainly sharpens the senses and the intellect, *is* real education.

Parents should always be pleased to see their children play. They should provide a secure environment for this purpose and, whenever possible, join in the fun.

Mind Matters

Mind Matters

Unbelievable challenge

Suppose a scientist invents a device that straps to your head and accurately works out what you do and don't believe. He issues a challenge to the public: after measuring a volunteer's beliefs, he will pick one belief and ask the volunteer to change it. If they manage to do so, they will win £1,000,000.

You decide to accept this challenge. When you arrive, the scientist places the device on your head, and within seconds informs you that you believe your car is red. You are amazed at the accuracy of his machine. Your car is indeed red and you believe it is. He then asks you to believe instead that your car is *blue*.

Would you be able to meet this challenge and win the money? Do you think that, if you tried hard enough, you would be able to convince yourself and truly believe that your car isn't red, but blue? If not, why not? Aren't you are in charge of your own psychological state?

In some religions, those who do not believe in God are threatened with the punishment of hellfire. But if we have no choice about our beliefs, can this punishment be justified?

Skeletons in the closet

Case 1

I have a fear of human skeletons, be they in the laboratory, horror films or graveyards. I once reminded myself of the obvious, which I had never contemplated before:

"I needn't feel scared of skeletons. After all, I have always lived with one – my own!"

Should this reminder help to overcome my fear, or should it make my situation even worse, forcing me to think of myself as being accompanied by a skeleton all the time, wherever I go?

Case 2

I used to be afraid of the dark – nights were terrifying for me. But what if I had reminded myself of the obvious, which I'd never contemplated before:

"I needn't feel scared of darkness," I might have thought. "After all, I have always lived with it. Light never goes beyond our retinas, which are part of our eyes, so our brains always remain in the dark, be it day or night!"

Should this reminder have helped me to overcome my fear, or should it have made my situation even worse, forcing me to think of myself as being in perpetual darkness?

Unshaven or ungrown?

"You'd better shave. You haven't shaved for two days now," my wife reprimanded me one day.

"Look at that man over there. He hasn't shaved for at least two years!" I replied, trying to justify myself.

"But he's got a beard, silly," my wife retorted.

"Ah, but while he was *growing* his beard, his face must have been like mine, at one stage," I reasoned.

"But you are not planning to grow a beard, are you?"

"True, but how would anyone else know that?" I replied.

Defending against your conscience

All of us are endowed with a mysterious inner voice that guides us in moral matters. I am sure there is such a concept in every culture. In English, it is called 'conscience'; the Urdu word for this entity is *'zameer'*.

In Urdu it is often said that someone's zameer has died, is asleep or has woken up. However, I believe our conscience is always alive and awake – despite our best efforts, sometimes, to ignore it! We have all sorts of ways to deceive it or bypass it. We try to avoid the watchful eyes of our conscience by making excuses. Most people who commit even criminal acts claim to have some sort of justification. Such is human ingenuity.

Let's suppose a man finds a wallet lying on the footpath. He picks it up and finds that it contains £100 in cash, together with the name and address of the owner. His conscience tells him that he ought to return the wallet. However, he can think of countless more or less unconscionable excuses to avoid this moral tug and keep the money for himself:

- "When I lost *my* wallet last year, no one returned it."
- "If he hadn't lost it, he'd have spent it by now anyway."
- "Maybe it's not his money. He could have stolen it."
- "It must belong to some miser. He needs this punishment."
- "He's already gone through the pain of his loss. There's no point in letting him suffer in vain."
- "He could have spent it on gambling or other wrongdoings, so he should be happy he lost it. And I'm happy I found it, so we're both happy. We should both be thankful to God."
- "Nature's ways are mysterious. There must be some hidden reason for this event. Nature knows who is needy and who isn't; otherwise this wouldn't have happened."
- "He might very well have been the one that found my wallet last year – who knows? This money was mine."
- "God will give him more, that's my prayer."

Humbled by greatness

Once, when I was helping my daughter Rushda with her physics homework, she said to me, “Dad, you know so much science!”

“Oh no,” I replied modestly. “I am like Newton playing with pebbles on the sea-shore, while the great ocean of truth lies all undiscovered before me.”

Rushda raised her eyebrows. Was I really being humble?

Worry and regret

Is it rational to worry about something which is inevitable, such as death; or to regret some event in our life which is now long past?

The inevitable will happen, regardless of what we do. And the past remains unchanged, regardless of our regrets. It seems to me that worry or regret about that over which we have no control can only be irrational. The fact remains, however, that we do still worry and regret. Why is this?

The punch-line

Humour often relies on misdirection and anticipation followed by a surprising ending. A joke would cease to be funny if you put the punch-line first, and then went over the ground leading up to it.

Suppose you are in Heaven telling a good joke to God and some of your fellow souls. The misdirection and surprise would work on the others, but not at all on God, who can see all things at once, and knows the punch-line before you have even got under way. The apparent conclusion is that God would be the only one there not to get the joke.

My prayer

Dear God,
Please do not give me wisdom in hindsight;
Give me wisdom in foresight.
Then I won't need wisdom in hindsight.

Don't forget

During the course of a day, we switch the lights on and off in our houses very many times. Of course, several times a day, someone forgets to switch a light off. But, interestingly, hardly anyone ever forgets to switch a light on!

Similarly, we rarely forget to take our umbrellas out with us, but we often forget to bring them back.

What do such cases tell us about ourselves? It looks as though it might be human to forget about things we don't immediately need. We should try not to allow this approach to characterise our dealings with people as well. Don't forget!

F***ing hypocrites

I have often felt bemused by the use of asterisks to censor what we write. Can there be any doubt in the reader's mind concerning what I mean when I write 'f***ing' above?

Given that almost all readers are certain of precisely what the word is, and precisely which letter is meant by each asterisk, why on earth should readers frown if I write the word in its full, naked and uncensored form?

More to the point, why would I *myself* think that using the asterisks above, instead of letters, has enhanced the quality of this book? Or hasn't it?

For the record, the obscured word above is 'fooling'.

Don't read this title

Are we, or are we not, in control of our own minds? This may seem a strange question; and stranger still if I suggest that in some situations our own minds will work to thwart our intentions! Consider the following story.

A man went to see a *Sunyasee*, that is, a witch-doctor, to learn his recipe for making gold. The Sunyasee gave him a list of the weird ingredients to be used and told him how to combine them, and after ten minutes the man turned to leave, dreaming now of becoming the richest man on Earth.

"Just a moment," the Sunyasee warned. "There is one further matter to point out, a simple precaution you must take if the recipe is to be successful."

"No problem. What is it?" said the man, still beaming with happiness.

"The thought of a monkey must never cross your mind during the whole procedure!" the Sunyasee advised, a knowing look on his face.

A fairy tale

Once upon a time, there was a woman, Rose, who was in love with a man, Jack. However, everyone knew that Jack loved Jill, another woman from the town. For this reason, day in day out, Rose's heart was near breaking.

One day, Jack had an accident on the hillside. Although he emerged otherwise unscathed, his head was badly knocked, with the result that he began to believe Rose was Jill, and Jill was Rose. The two had swapped places in his head.

This mismatch became quickly apparent, when Jack referred to Jill as 'Rose', and to Rose as 'Jill'. But Jack's doctors came to the wrong – though more obvious – diagnosis. They told Jack that, as a result of his accident, he had swapped the *names* of the two women in his head – as opposed to the entire persons! To put matters right, they told him to swap the names back, and call Rose 'Rose', and Jill 'Jill'.

So from then on Rose received all the love from Jack that she had always dreamed of – all the love that Jack would, but for the accident, have continued to give to Jill. And Rose was blissfully unaware that Jack had mistaken her identity, as he continued to call her 'Rose'.

Jack and Rose married, and Jack was a devoted husband. However, one day, Rose realised Jack thought she was Jill, and it all came tumbling down. Rose immediately banished Jack from the house, filed for divorce, and returned to her fits of heartbreak. Would you have done the same as Rose?

You decide the moral of the story.

Dream ticket

I once saw a good Indian film with a friend of mine. When I met him again after a few days, I told him that I had seen the film again, though this time in a dream.

"Lucky you," he jested. "So you didn't just see it again. You saw it for free!"

"Oh no, no. I still had to buy a ticket!" I told him seriously.

Appearance and reality

It is certain that the way the world *looks* to us is a separate thing from the way it really *is*. This presents the following possibilities:

- The real world is more beautiful than it appears.
- The real world is less beautiful than it appears.
- The real world is as beautiful as it appears.

Which state of affairs above would you prefer? In a nutshell, what is more important for you and why: appearance or reality?

Opposite conclusions

It is often possible to say something which means the complete opposite of the way it's likely to be understood. For example:

> *"My hair is no longer falling."*

You might suppose that the person saying this has found a cure for his hair loss. In truth, he has become completely bald! Or again:

> *"I no longer need to wear any glasses."*

Has the speaker regained normal eyesight? In fact, he has gone completely blind!

Mad world?

If the whole world looks upside down to you, then you are definitely standing upside down on your head.

This same lesson ought to be learnt in many other matters. If the whole world seems insane, you are probably mad. If the whole world seems evil, you are probably malign. If the whole world seems a dull place, you are probably a dull person.

A messy situation

Someone has a very high opinion of you, and therefore doesn't allow you to use his mucky bathroom, for fear of what you might think of him. However, someone else has a very low opinion of you, and does allow you to use his mucky bathroom, because he couldn't care less about you, and what you might think about him. Given that you are desperate to go to the bathroom, which of these two persons do *you* have the higher opinion of?

What to do with a crook-lock

I used to have a very old car, one that would have been difficult to sell. When it was stolen one day, I was greatly relieved at the thought that with the help of the insurance I would be able to buy a decent replacement. But my hopes were dashed when the police found my jalopy after just a few days, and I had to go to collect it.

I did not suffer just one such disappointment. Four or five times my car was taken by joyriders and then found abandoned, and the police would ring me to tell me its location. I do not believe that the police were especially efficient; simply that the thieves very soon realised that they had made a serious mistake. Their anger was expressed in the way they treated the car before abandoning it, so that on each occasion I would find it vandalised, and a lot of money and effort would be needed to put it right.

Eventually I became completely fed up with such annoying episodes. One day, when I was going to work in the newly recovered car, I decided to put a stop to all the hassle, once and for all. I parked the car and rushed off to buy a sturdy looking crook-lock. However, when I arrived back at the spot where I had parked, I found to my utmost horror that the car was missing once again!

As if this wasn't enough, an additional problem arose as to what to do with the big crook-lock. I stood there looking silly with the thing in my hands. It was already getting late, and I had to be at work quite soon. But I found a nice solution to my problem: I didn't want to haul such a bulky object all the way to the office, so I locked it around a nearby lamp post before setting off, and left the lamp post to stand guard while I was away.

A little boy had been watching me with interest. Noticing his gaze, I told him that I was making sure no one came and stole the lamp post. When I eventually returned later in the day, I found the lamp post intact, but the crook-lock had disappeared.

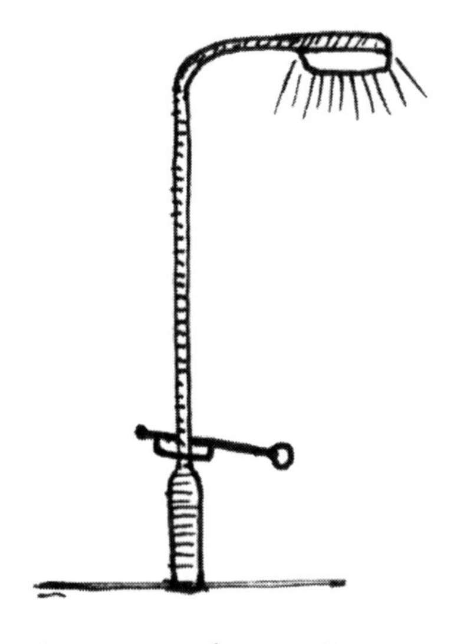

A very secure lamp post

Cold comfort

An unexpected lady visitor once went upstairs to use our bathroom. Rashid, my visiting relative, was having a shower in there at the time, and he hadn't thought there was any need to lock the bathroom door.

"She just barged straight in, without knocking, while I was having a shower!" he exclaimed, later on. "Thank God, she didn't see me naked. I had soap all over my body."

A very interesting question

I once attended a lecture by a prominent philosopher. Halfway through, I asked him a question which took some time for me to explain. I sat expectantly, awaiting his response.

After some time, the lecturer spoke. "That's a *very* interesting question!" he said. "Thanks for bringing it up!"

I beamed with pride. My query had been thoroughly appreciated by a well-respected philosopher! In fact, I felt so appreciated that it wasn't until I got home that I realised he hadn't gone on to answer my question at all!

How to read 'How to Read a Book'

I have come across a book entitled *How to Read a Book*. This title got me thinking.

If I can read the book, then clearly I already know how to read a book, and so I don't need to read it. If I can't read it, then nor can I learn from it how to read a book. So whether or not I can read it, the book cannot help me. *How to Read a Book* cannot in fact teach me how to read a book.

Did the author of *How to Read a Book* previously fail to read *How to Write a Book*?

Repetition repetition repetition repetition repetition

Familiarity is the result of repetition. We are most familiar with the people whom we see the most. However, an overdose can have the opposite effect.

If you stare continuously at a picture of someone you know well, you will find that after a while they start to become less and less familiar, even if you're looking at a photograph of yourself! Similarly with a word you know well, repeating it over and over, and over, and over, and over again, can often make it sound strange. I wonder why this is so?

Great expectations

The need to come up to other people's expectations can have a great influence on the way a person acts, sometimes for good, sometimes not. There are many contexts in which this is true, ranging from the academic to the social. Let me illustrate what I mean with three examples.

Example 1

I once praised a young man in front of him to another person. I knew that the young man had started to smoke, but the young man didn't know that I knew.

I said, "There's such a lot of pressure on young people these days to get into bad habits, smoking and the like. Fortunately, they don't all succumb. Take our young friend here for example. He doesn't give in to pressure from his peers! I've never seen him smoke a single cigarette."

And I never did see the boy smoke. After my praise, he either gave up smoking, or took pains to avoid confronting me while doing so.

Example 2

Parents often have great expectations of their children, particularly where academic pursuits are concerned. However, these expectations can often have a debilitating effect on performance. If the expectations are too high, the child will feel unable to reach them.

On the other hand, if parental expectations are too low the child might have no incentive to achieve their full potential. So the problem for the parent is to have just the right expectations.

I'm afraid that the more I think about this, the more complicated it seems, and the more difficult it becomes to form any sort of expectation at all.

Example 3

I was once jogging in the local park late on a winter evening. It was very quiet.

All of a sudden, about five Asian youths appeared on their bikes from nowhere. They stopped me and moments later I found myself surrounded by them. From their remarks and threatening behaviour, I knew I was in trouble.

"You're all alone here. Don't you feel scared?" one youth probed, as they all edged closer.

"Scared?" I replied with confidence, as if the idea was preposterous. "With so many tough young men from my own country around me, there's no need to be scared of white racists here!"

They quickly went into reverse gear.

"Of course not, Uncle!" one said.

"Goodnight!" someone else said.

And they zoomed away on their bikes, apparently pleased to have been able to make me feel safe.

Why do expectations cast such a magic spell?

A reason to believe in reason

Any rational person knows the importance of reason. The need to be reasonable is becoming even more pressing in the present explosive political climate of the world.

Reason enables us to see each other's point of view, to allay each other's misunderstandings, and to resolve our differences. However, this is only possible if *both* parties are reasonable.

The trouble is that we don't know how to impart a belief in the value of reason to those who do not share that belief, without using reason itself. Rationality has always had an uphill struggle against Ignorance, and without a new approach perhaps it always will.

A different approach to sales

I wanted to buy a new kettle, and went into the local superstore where I found two I liked. As far as I could see they were identical, except that one was priced at £27 and the other at £19. A young salesman approached me, who seemed to be newly appointed, and the following conversation ensued.

"Can I help you, sir?"

"What's the difference between these two?" I asked.

He examined them closely and carefully for a little while.

"This one's twenty-seven pounds, and that one's nineteen pounds," he said at last.

"Oh, I know what they cost. I want to know the *difference* between them."

"I see what you mean," he said. Then he took out his calculator, typed in some figures and eventually announced "The difference is eight pounds." After this little surprise, I decided not to pursue the matter.

A matter of opinion

Suppose you want to get rid of someone's company for good, someone who holds you in high esteem for some quality of yours. Would you be prepared to convince them that they had been mistaken about you, in order to keep them away?

Would a woman be prepared to present herself at her very worst, in order to put off an unwelcome suitor?

I wonder why we would wish to avoid the low opinion of someone of whom our own opinion is the lowest.

The naked truth

If you speak on the telephone to someone of the opposite sex, does it matter whether either of you has any clothes on? If not, then why should you feel unwilling to mention your nakedness to the person to whom you are speaking?

The importance of samosas

Your friend and you are at someone's house, where you are offered some delicious *samosas*. Both you and your friend love samosas, but you discover that your friend is unable to eat them that evening on account of a minor stomach upset.

You are unhappy that your friend is deprived of such good food. But on the other hand, you're happy you have twice as many for yourself!

On balance, which is greater – the happiness or the sadness? Your answer will determine just how important samosas are for you.

Samosas

Was the wrong diagnosis right?

Suppose a man has an irrational fear that the roof of his house will fall on him, and suppose that his wife arranges for the doctor to visit. After several tests, the doctor tells him that his fear is in fact only due to a mineral deficiency in his brain.

If the man believes in science and trusts his doctor, his fear might very well evaporate in the light of the pronouncement, even though the mineral deficiency remains. If so, are we to say that the doctor gave the wrong diagnosis, but was right to do so?

The pain of gain

A man went out with empty pockets, and came back with £900, but was very unhappy!

When asked by his wife why he was looking glum, he told her that on his walk he had found a roll of bank-notes totalling £1,000, hidden behind a tree. But in his rush to get home, he had accidentally dropped £100 of it somewhere on his way. His fortune had been decimated in an instant – what a loss! His wife tried to comfort him but to no avail.

Later on, the man went out again. He was still unhappy about his previous loss. He found the same lucky tree as before, and started searching around, looking for the £100 he had dropped. To his great astonishment, behind a nearby rock he found another wad of £1,000. He put it into his pocket and made his way home. However, he remained unhappy!

When he arrived home his wife asked him why he was sad. The man explained that his fortune now stood at £1,900. If he had not lost that £100, he would have had £2,000 by now!

But his wife pointed out something he hadn't yet considered. If, instead of finding the second £1,000, he had come across the original £100 that he had lost, he would by now have been quite happy. He had to agree with what his wife said, but this didn't make him feel any better. For him, unhappiness took precedence over logic.

Another fairy tale

After the divorce, Jack suddenly found himself cured. Once again he knew Jill to be Jill and Rose to be Rose – and consequently he became glad about the separation!

Rose still loved Jack, and she wanted him to be happy. However, Jack could only be happy if Jill was happy. The problem was, in her jealousy, Rose would be unhappy if Jill was happy. How should Rose feel?

You decide the ending of the story.

Caught in the middle

I used to play table-tennis every week with my good friend Richard. Eventually, another friend of ours, Altaf, joined us. It has to be said that Altaf was, relatively speaking, a beginner.

To start with, when Richard or I played with Altaf, we gave him a lot of consideration. By adopting a level of play just above his, we gave him a lot of good practice. However, after a few weeks, he found that he started to get more and more soundly defeated by each of us.

His erstwhile considerate teachers had been changing into aggressive opponents, each intent on giving him as crushing a defeat as we could. Not only that, but eventually we each started giving him twice as many games, because, without realising it, we did not feel the need to play with each other anymore.

Some weeks later, Altaf apologised for not being able to give us interesting games, as his play was getting worse and worse. In a flash, I realised what had been going on. Without thinking, I shared this insight with Altaf.

"Don't worry," I said. "We are not playing these games with you. I've just realised, that's only an illusion. In actual fact, Richard and I have been competing with each other – to see who can give you the more crushing defeat!"

Altaf didn't seem at all pleased with the shared insight, and he stopped coming round soon after that. Without his presence, Richard and I found that the game had lost its spice, and getting back to normal was difficult.

Investing in exercise

From the obituaries of the famous that I read in *The Times*, I can see that they generally die younger than they should. From this it seems to me that they have probably spent too much time on their interests, and not enough on looking after their physical wellbeing! Perhaps we should take a lesson from this.

Some people might object that they enjoy all of their time, and have no time left for exercise. However, this cannot be true. We all waste *some* time every day doing nothing enjoyable. To exercise in this time would be no loss. But equally, to spend *all* our time exercising would certainly be a waste!

We should realise that investing just a little time in our health can greatly enhance our lifespan, giving us more time, not only for our interests, but also for enjoying a well earned retirement. Are we not being irrational when we fail to spend, say, just 30 minutes a day on exercise, when the result could even be another 30 years of healthy living?

Heartbreaking films

Scientists have found evidence supporting claims made about the healing power of laughter, claims to the effect that laughter appears to help to keep the heart beating strongly by improving arterial blood flow. Apparently, the impact on your heart of watching a very funny film is equivalent to an hour or so in the gym! However, it is not the improvement to our health that makes us value such films, it is the laughter. And this is understandable.

On the other hand, it is much more difficult to understand why so many people, including me, like to see films, indeed pay to see films, that make them sad. There is no scientific evidence to suggest that there is any health value in unhappiness. So, why do we like sad films?

The answer that might be given is that the situation in the film is not real but simulated, and that the unhappiness it induces is not real either. Well, all right. But the question now becomes: how is it that the better the simulation, and the closer it is to real unhappiness, the better are the ratings of the film, and the more it is 'enjoyed' by those who watch it?

The value of a belief

Is a belief the kind of thing that can be valuable? Surely there is only one measure of value for a belief: whether or not it is true. But, rather than cherish true beliefs, people often take the truth of their cherished beliefs for granted, and defend them at all costs.

Suppose you have a cherished but mistaken belief. Can you hold fast to your belief in spite of evidence to the contrary? Perhaps you believe the world is flat, but are also aware that modern science disagrees. By making necessary changes here and there, you can rescue your belief, if you cherish it. For example, you could start believing that science isn't to be trusted.

Global conflict is a case in point. Every nation has its own beliefs, be these political, ethical or religious. Where these beliefs conflict, not everyone can be right. Despite this, no one will stand down. It seems as though it is more important for a nation to safeguard its core beliefs than seek out the truth of the matter.

Mysteries of Life
and
the Universe

Mysteries of Life and the Universe

The conscious Universe

'Nature', taking a broad perspective, is just our word for the Universe and the way it works. Whatever is happening in the Universe, Nature is doing it.

Nature is self-aware, because we are self-aware, and we are a part of Nature just like every other physical thing. We are the consciousness of the Universe. But the consciousness of the Universe does not depend on it containing a vast number of conscious creatures – just one is enough to make the entire Universe a conscious entity.

Given that I know there is a table in front of me, Nature knows it too; and given that Stephen Hawking knows that spiral nebulae recede from each other as the Universe expands, Nature knows it. Through us, Nature ponders about itself and writes about itself. When Nature creates a beautiful valley, Nature admires itself and paints itself.

Although I'm attracted by this unified view of Nature, it isn't always so awe-inspiring. Sometimes, Nature even appears as though She has to correct Her own mistakes. One example comes from my personal experience: on the one hand Nature deteriorated my eyesight, but then She provided me with glasses!

Questions about Matter, Space and Time

These three concepts are fundamental to the way we understand reality. But even a simple question on these topics is an Ultimate Question.

- What is matter?
- What is space?
- What is time?

These are the most obvious questions of all, but maybe we'll never have any satisfactory answers.

Most of our concepts, even if quite vague, can be tested by asking questions. For instance, to clarify our concept of *life*, we might ask whether life begins at birth or before, or whether plants are truly alive.

In this way, we can arrive at an approximation of the concept we are seeking. If we try this technique with matter, space and time, however, we immediately find ourselves plunging into deep waters.

The following questions are just a few of those that suggest themselves.

- Are matter, space and time infinitely divisible? Or is there a 'smallest amount' of matter, space and time?
- Can matter exist without space, that is, could the Universe be jam-packed with matter all the way up to infinity?
- Could the Universe consist only of space and no matter?
- If the Universe did contain just space, could there be time?
- Could there be a one-particle universe, with no other space than that containing the particle?
- If the Universe contained just one fundamental particle, could there be time?

Stopping and starting

I once saw a woodlouse walking across the floor. I must have frightened it in some way, for it stopped in its tracks, and remained quite still. I was watching closely all the while. Silently, I kept it under constant surveillance.

Five minutes later, it suddenly walked off again. There was no physical cause that I could discern, though, of course, it seems unlikely that it would have remained stationary indefinitely. With no external cause available to explain its departure, we must infer an internal one. But what kind of cause might this be? Only a woodlouse could tell me.

Even now, ten years later, I am still mystified as to just what prompted it to resume its journey. Where it was going to is a separate mystery altogether.

Wrath of a Mad God

I recently saw an advertisement for a novel entitled *Wrath of a Mad God*. This title got me thinking.

Wrath of a Mad God?

Not even the most unrelenting horror film could possibly capture the scenario that this title conjures. First concentrate individually on the ideas 'Wrath', 'Mad' and 'God'. Now combine them.

Proving a negative

It is much easier to show that something is the case than to show that it is not. To show that bananas exist, it is enough to find a banana. This is the end of the demonstration. However, to show that bananas do not exist, it is not enough to fail to find any, for who knows where a banana might be hiding? There is no end to this quest.

If God exists we'll eventually be able to discover Him. But if God doesn't exist, we'll never know He doesn't.

The invisible hand

Religious eyes see the Universe as a purposeful place. What goes on can be explained in terms of purposes and goals. For example, water evaporates from the seas, and in the form of clouds it irrigates distant places across the world. It is as though a great, invisible hand is lifting water from where it is plentiful, and depositing it where it is needed for the survival of mankind.

I find myself swept along by this image, until I recall that there are many places which are completely missed out by the invisible hand, and which as a result turn into deserts. I think also of the fact that most of the rain falls on the sea, where it is not needed at all.

Not so weedy after all

We recently had tarmac laid on our front garden path and firmly pressed down with a heavy roller. The tarmac hardened in a few days.

A few weeks later, we noticed that one spot on the path was slightly cracked, and heaving upwards. The following morning, I found that the tarmac at that spot had split open and, to my surprise, a tiny delicate weed was peeping through!

How could such a tiny and delicate plant ever bring about such an upheaval, and cause such damage to our footpath?

The human body

Many things are remarkable about the human body. Take something as small as a capillary – a tiny vessel through which blood cells move in *single file*. How did the two adapt over time to each other's relative sizes? What was going on before this happened?

The body almost seems to *understand* itself. When we are wounded, thousands of capillaries – along with nerve fibres and other cells – are damaged. However, the body is able to rebuild and rearrange these cells and *reconnect* all our capillaries. How do the vast number of veins (carrying used-up blood cells) and arteries (carrying oxygenated blood) connect up correctly, so that the whole of the affected area is 'irrigated' after the healing process is complete?

Our lungs transfer oxygen into the bloodstream through a network of millions of capillaries. The number of these capillaries increases after birth until maturity, and our lungs increase in size while keeping the same shape. How does the network of capillaries continue to build up, while the lungs keep on breathing without a pause?

Road and train networks are generally disrupted while they are being extended. But this isn't the case with our lungs. Everything continues to function properly and there is no disruption to normal services. We continue about our daily lives oblivious to the miracles taking place within us.

What does getting old mean?

The fundamental particles of matter never become aged. An electron today is exactly the same as it was at the time of the Big Bang. When *we* get old, our particles don't. So what does getting old really mean? And why do we get old at all, if what we are made of doesn't?

The moving finger

I can move my finger as and when I like, and I take its movement for granted. Yet I don't know how I do it.

In order to move my finger I must first think about moving my finger. But how do I manage to convert my intangible thought into a tangible result? It must be more complicated than simply *thinking* about it. I can think, "move, finger" right now, and yet my finger does not move. So what else is required?

What would happen if I woke one morning to find I had forgotten how to move my finger? It seems clear to me that no one would be able to help me, not even world famous neuroscientists! Nor would I be able to help them to help me, despite my privileged access to my own brain. What a frightening thought! Perhaps you can help me. Can you explain exactly what I have to do to get my finger to move?

Doctor knows best?

"I'm here for my scheduled check-up, Doctor," said the patient.

"No problem," said the doctor, connecting a device. "I can tell you are in pain."

"Actually, doctor, the pain has gone away since you gave me that medicine last time. Thanks ever so much."

"No, no, no, no, no," said the doctor with great concern. "My test shows clearly that you are experiencing excruciating pain at this very moment. I must prescribe you some stronger painkillers."

"Honestly, doctor, I'm quite fine. There's no pain whatsoever!"

"Look, kid," said the doctor, becoming exasperated. "I'm the one with the PhD, not you. My analysis of the data was quite thorough. You are definitely most uncomfortable."

"But doctor," the patient exclaimed. "I assure you –"

"That's quite enough," interrupted the doctor. "You're quite mistaken. The pain is intense. You will have to continue with the medicine."

"Okay..." the patient said, unsure what to think, and unwilling to question the doctor's expertise. "So I'll let you know when the pain has subsided?"

"No," retorted the doctor. "*I'll* let *you* know when the pain has subsided."

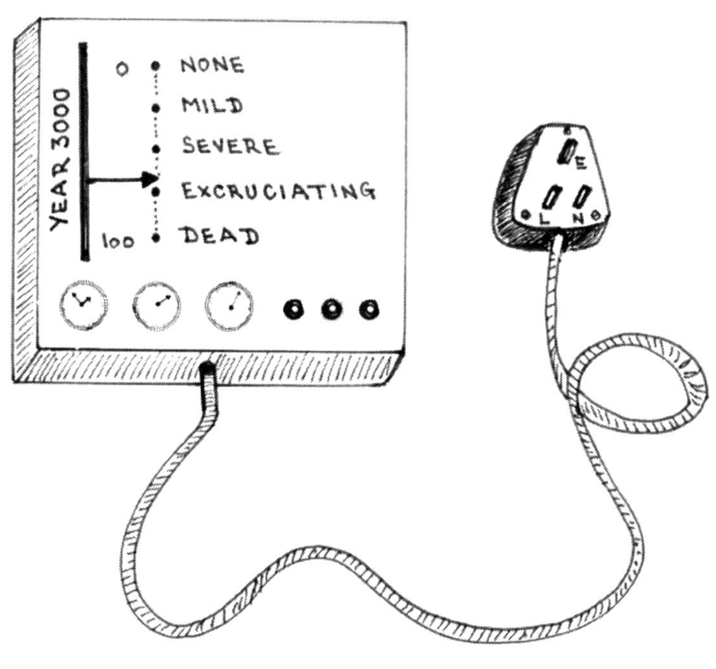

Painometer™ Z60

The extent of loss

Suppose that if you were to die naturally of old age, you would die at 90, but that you were murdered when you were only 50. You would thereby have lost 40 years of your life.

Would this loss of 40 years be a *permanent loss* or would it come to an end 40 years after your death, when you would have died anyway?

The uniqueness of experiences

"You cannot step twice into the same river."

Heraclitus

Certain experiences are such that we yearn to relive them. For instance, I remember fondly the first time I learnt to ride a bike. However, no matter how many times I ride a bike today, I can never again experience the first exhilaration of the balancing act and being carried along on two wheels. No two experiences can ever be identical.

For this reason, no two people can ever truly share an experience. Even if two people experience one event, they both look upon it from different angles and react to it in different ways. When we say we have shared an experience, we do not mean more than that we meddled with the same bit of objective reality.

Memories of sensations

Think of the last time you ate an apple. You can remember its colour and its shape. You remember how it felt in your hand, and the texture of its skin. You can remember its smell and its taste as you bit it, and the sound of the crunch.

But its colour, shape, texture, smell, taste and sound are not currently present, because the apple is not present. How is it then that you are still 'experiencing' it?

How is that that the properties – so intrinsically possessed by an apple – can exist in our brains? Given that nothing within our brain is in the least like an apple, what is it in our brains that relates to this fruit?

No one observing my brain, with whatever form of scanner that might be devised, will ever actually observe what I experience as a recollection of the apple. So, in what form within my brain are my sensations of the apple stored?

Clever tongues

If Nature were to reward any organ at all, it ought to be our acrobatic tongue for its dual role in the activities of speaking and eating.

When we speak, thoughts come from the brain above, while the throat, together with the lungs, produces vowel sounds from below – and the tongue sorts it all out in the middle. Notice how quickly the tongue twists and turns as we speak, to translate our thoughts into intelligible expressions for others!

When we eat, our tongue works in a very hostile environment. Our jaws and teeth apparently try incredibly hard to supplement our meal and turn the tongue into mincemeat. But the tongue moves with an adroitness which is hard to explain, and always manages to survive the attacks unscathed – or nearly always!

It is amazing that the tongue and the teeth have learnt to play this dangerous game, while we sit back and enjoy our meal.

One week to live

Suppose it was discovered that the world would come to an end in one week's time, and suppose also that there is no after-life. What would you do?

Would you seek all the thrills and pleasant experiences you could have, before the end came? Would you experiment with hallucinogenic drugs? If you were on the top of the Eiffel Tower in the last seconds, would you make the most of your location so as to experience the ultimate thrill of sky-diving without a parachute?

If not, why not?

Opposable thumbs

During its formation, cataclysmic upheavals raged across the primordial Earth. Suppose that some alien race visiting the early planet at the time dropped some things on the surface before they left – a needle and thread, and a deflated balloon.

Is it even remotely possible that, during this period of chaos, the balloon could get inflated and then knotted? Due to some violent movements, atmospheric pressures and powerful winds, could the needle get threaded? What would be the chance of such an event?

Four billion years later on, we perform both acts with the utmost ease, barely thinking about it at all. Suppose the aliens return sometime after the end of the human race, and see a knotted balloon – what would they think?

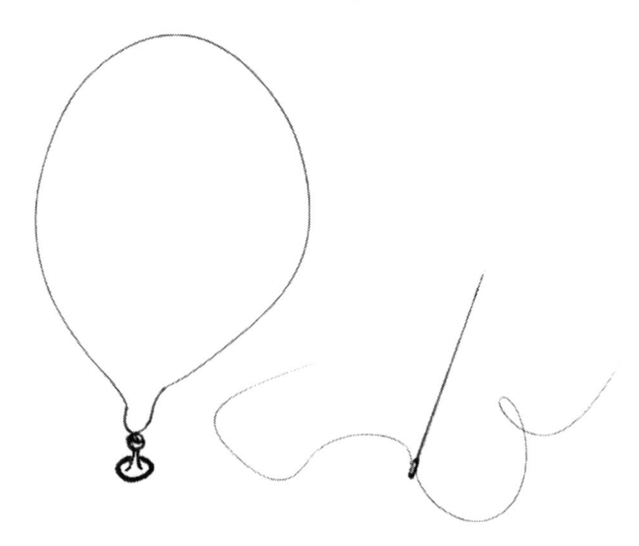

Consciousness and survival

The survival of our own species depends vitally upon the fact that we are conscious of what we do. With other species, the very opposite can be the case. If spiders were conscious, they would be quite unable to reproduce the webs of their ancestors, upon which they depend for survival. In fact, their dependence upon complex instinctive behaviour for survival must work against the appearance of consciousness in their future evolution. As soon as any spider started to think about what it was doing, it would cease to be able to do it.

Making sense of the world

Why did we develop exactly five senses: sight, hearing, touch, smell and taste? It is not because they are sufficient to experience all the qualities of objects in the world, for we know there are plenty of qualities that we do not experience through our senses.

So, is it that we only need five senses in order to survive? If so, do you think that this will remain the case forever? Wouldn't it be interesting if the human race, at some stage in its development, acquired additional sensory apparatus with which to experience the world – an extra eye in the back of the head perhaps, or even a completely new sense altogether?

Survival instinct

You can't teach a newly born baby anything straight away. But fortunately the most important skill is innate. Babies try to gobble up any part of their environment that happens to be passing at the time, regardless of its size and of the size of their mouth – even dogs or cats will do! Some of this behaviour might be inappropriate and need to be discouraged. But the innate compulsion to place everything into their mouths and spit out what doesn't taste nice is necessary for survival.

Trouble can arise because the inspection process is not perfect, and unhealthy or oversized items can pass though the mouth without being rejected. It is here that parents fit into the picture, their role being to ensure that only safe items get into baby in the first place.

'Mama' and 'Papa'

My little grandson Rehan has just learned to say 'Mama' and 'Papa'. There is a good reason to regard it as very curious that infants can do this. Although these two words are often the first to be articulated by a child, no adult finds it easy to articulate what the difference is, in terms of physical movements within the mouth, that determines which of the two quite distinct words comes out.

It is easy to say 'Ma' and it is easy to say 'Pa'. I have no doubt that an expert in phonetics would be able to explain the subtly different ways these two sounds are produced. But children have no need of expert explanations and diagrams. They just go ahead and talk.

Children never mix up their Ma's and their Pa's, even though these sounds are produced in almost indistinguishable ways. And just to prove to you that they have it right, they repeat them as well. Not just 'Ma' but 'Mama'. Not just 'Pa' but 'Papa'. They never say 'Mapa' and they never say 'Pama'.

The circle of life

When I was in town one Saturday, I saw a throng of people milling around the shops. I thought to myself: "In a hundred and fifty years, all of them will have been replaced by new people. They too will be milling around, and no one will have noticed a difference. In fact, every single person I can see right now, including me, will then be dead, and yet no one will think anything of it!"

If they all died together, the event would certainly be a human tragedy. But what difference does it make whether they all die together, or die one by one as in fact they do?

If there is no difference, it seems that all of life is nothing less than a gradual tragedy. In fact, this tragedy must have been going on for thousands and thousands of years without anyone noticing, until the author of *The Logic of Half a Moustache* looked into it!

An evolutionary mystery

According to the Theory of Evolution, all species have evolved through a process of natural selection. Isn't it bizarre that, as a result of this, with the development of intelligence and the ability to reflect, a member of one of those species discovered the origin of species? In other words, even the discovery of evolution was a result of evolution. I find this particular fact to be even more amazing than the theory.

A slug's reflections

A slug was pondering the mysteries of life and the Universe:

"I might be very slow, but at least my speed is greater than zero.

"So, if I could go on long enough, and was able to survive, I could even cross the whole of the Universe.

"But what would be the point? What is the point of life, anyway?"

He heaved a great sigh, curled up, and went to sleep.

We are all stardust

At the time of the Big Bang, the Universe was smaller than a pinhead, if we are to believe the cosmologists. The whole Universe, which now spans billions of light-years across, was closer to us then than most of our body parts are to each other right now.

Bearing this in mind, we should see great unity among all of mankind. The stuff on the original pinhead, of which we are formed, has gone through cataclysmic changes, and has existed in stars situated at colossal distances apart, long before the Earth was formed. And yet here we are, together again on this tiny planet, after 15 billion years!

When two people – say, father and son, or two brothers – meet after 60 years of separation, we see headlines in newspapers together with pictures of their celebration. On the other hand, when the whole of humanity meets again after 15 billion years, it's completely ignored by the media! Given that 15 billion years ago we could hardly have been closer together, don't you think that we ought now to put aside our differences and celebrate our reunion with the gusto it deserves?

Forty New Puzzles with Answers

Forty New Puzzles with Answers

So far we have looked at plenty of puzzles without any definite answers. For a change, I now offer you 40 puzzles which definitely do have answers – though it is realised that these answers are not always unique. In such cases, it is hoped that readers will think of their own neat solutions.

If you want to come back to the puzzles later, you can skip straight to the *Epilogue* at the end of the book, on page 209.

Meeting in the forest

In the middle of the night, a man is sitting alone in a forest which spreads for miles around him. A female stranger comes along, and sits down next to him. They exchange no greetings whatsoever, and after 10 minutes or so she takes out a sandwich from her bag and eats it. After about half an hour she gets up and leaves. No word has been spoken between them.

This may seem very strange, but in fact it is a common scenario. Can you explain what is going on?

See page 199

Cook's surprise

It has to be admitted that I don't know how to cook. But my wife, I am pleased to say, suffers from no such deficiency. After several years of culinary bliss, I once asked her where she had learnt to cook so well.

Her answer took me by surprise.

"I learnt it from you!" she said without further explanation. For a minute I thought she was joking, but no! She was speaking truthfully.

Can you explain her apparently paradoxical remark?

See page 200

Finger strength

One day, my daughter – who was then 10 years old – went on a walk with me. While we were out, I raised her to 6 feet off the ground, using only my right index finger for power. How did I do it?

See page 201

Transportation feat

Five objects were lying in the road. Each was too heavy for me to carry, and too jagged and irregular to roll. But, using a piece of string, I single-handedly moved all of them 500 yards down the road, and the journey took only a minute. How did I do it?

See page 202

Tax relief

Genuine business expenses in the UK are eligible for tax relief. But my friend Karim told me there is one genuine business expense for which there is no tax relief. What is it?

See page 204

Phone upgrade

Someone had five children and all of them wanted their mobile phones to be upgraded. He bought just one new phone and managed to make them all happy! How did he do it?

See page 204

Multi-duty thermometer

Barometers measure atmospheric pressure and height. Thermometers measure temperature. How can you employ a thermometer to measure the height of a building?

See page 199

Disappearing act

What is it that, if it became bigger and bigger, it would suddenly disappear without a trace?

See page 200

Trading places

When I was standing in a queue inside a shop, I allowed the customer behind me to go first, and this helped us *both*. Can you explain?

See page 202

Moral problem

A moral philosopher was opposed to all rapes but one. In fact he was pleased that this particular rape took place. Why?

See page 203

Image quality

"Wow! Just look at that TV!" I said to my wife, pointing at a new model. "We really must buy it. The picture quality's superb – crystal-clear!"

"That is precisely why we don't need to buy it!" my wife remarked.

After some reflection I said, "Yes, of course!"

Why did we decide against buying the new model?

See page 204

Awkward shopkeeper

A friend of yours tells you about an extremely grumpy shopkeeper, who will do anything to make life difficult for his customers. Your friend relates that he recently took a faulty item back to the shop, and that even though he had his receipt, the grumpy shop-keeper refused to give him a refund.

On a later occasion you have to go to the same shop to return a similar item. Like your friend, you have the receipt. Unlike your friend, you already know that the shopkeeper will be obstructive.

Can you think of a good way to deal with the grumpy shopkeeper and obtain a refund?

See page 205

Portrait of the author

The photograph in the front of this book is a completely genuine photograph of the author. There was no image manipulation; if you had been there, you would have seen the author looking exactly as depicted. Can you make sense of how this photograph was taken?

See page 199

Clock speed

Normally the tip of the hour hand of a clock is moving much slower than that of the minute hand. Can you in principle adapt an accurate clock, without tampering with its mechanism, in such a way that the tip of the hour arm goes faster than the tip of the minute hand (or even faster than the tip of the second hand!) and yet the clock continues to give the correct time throughout the day?

See page 201

Coin puzzle

You are strolling in the woods on a Saturday evening when you come across a coin in the dirt. Returning home, some online research reveals that the coin is two thousand years old, and worth over £100,000. What is the most sensible thing you should do first thing on Monday morning?

See page 202

A pint of milk a day

Moriarty Junior, the master thief, stole a pint of milk from outside his neighbour's door every day for a month, without the milkman or the neighbour becoming suspicious. How did he do it?

See page 203

God cannot do certain logically possible tasks

God has infinite power, but most people agree that even He cannot do the logically impossible. He cannot make 2 and 2 equal 5, and nor can He make a triangle with four sides.

However, there are two *logically possible* tasks, let's say A and B, such that if God does A first, He can do B later; but if He does B first, He *can't* do A later!

Can you think of such an A and B?

See page 204

Proof that the Earth is stationary

When I was in Pakistan, I gave in to the temptation to buy a book entitled *Proof that the Earth is Stationary*. The author's 'proof' took some 100 pages for him to set out, but in essence it amounted to the following:

> *Fix a tube on a stand which is itself fixed to the Earth so that you can see the Pole Star through the tube. If you look through the fixed tube at any time of the year, you will still be able to see the Pole Star. We know that the Pole Star is stationary. So the Earth must be stationary.*

The author was conscientious. Given that his observations were accurate, where did he go wrong in his *reasoning*?

See page 206

Mirror, mirror

There is a part of your body which you cannot possibly touch with your index finger – but you can easily touch it in your image in the mirror. What part could this be?

See page 200

Spare change

My magazines and newspapers cost £4.19. I have 78 coins to the value of £5 in change in my pocket, as follows:

50p coins: 3
20p coins: 4
10p coins: 14
5p coins: 12
2p coins: 25
1p coins: 20

Understandably, when I pay, I want to get rid of as many of the coins as possible. How can I simplify the problem of which coins I should use?

See page 201

A total loss

You gained £20, and lost £21. How much was your total loss?

See page 202

The lecture effect

A man went to listen to a lecture by a visiting speaker at a university, at which some hundred people were present. The speaker was unknown to the man.

The man sat quietly throughout the lecture, which in no way offended him, contained no jokes and was relatively sober. But at one point the man's body chemistry changed and his heart started to race. He hadn't become ill, nor had anything dramatic occurred. What could have happened to put him into this state?

See page 203

Changing rooms

At a particular gym, the male and female changing rooms are exactly the same, other than the signs outside the doors. However, one day the management temporarily switched the signs around – men were told to use the Women's changing room, and women were told to use the Men's. This caused great inconvenience, but the management insisted it was necessary. Why could that be?

See page 204

Counting without counting

I asked someone to check that the number of objects in a box was 120. He looked uneasy for a while. Then he looked into the box and asked, "Are you sure there should be 120?"

"Yes, I'm quite sure," I replied.

He took away the box and saw me the following day.

"Yes, there are exactly 120," he said to me. Then, as he was leaving, he made a most surprising revelation. "I must admit," he said, "that I didn't count them at all. In fact, I've never learnt how to count. But you can rest assured, there are exactly 120. And I didn't get any help."

Given that there were indeed exactly 120 objects in the box, how did he check the number?

See page 207

Breaking the law

You see someone breaking the law. He deserves to be punished. But if you copy him you will not deserve to be punished. Indeed, if you don't follow suit the consequences will be very severe. What are we talking about here?

See page 200

Epistemological puzzle

I was shown a picture of what I was told to be a town and some of its surrounding landscape in Switzerland. When I looked at the picture, I didn't recognise it, or any of the features contained in it. There were no clues whatsoever in the picture itself to help me identify it. However, I knew that it was a picture of the town Davos. I was not guessing. I would not have been able to identify it without looking at the picture.

Why did I need to look at the picture, even though I did not recognise it? How could *seeing* a picture I did not recognise help me to discover that it was a picture of Davos?

See page 200

A race for 65's and over

An annual marathon race for senior citizens attracted hundreds of entries each year due to the excellent prizes up for grabs. The entry fee was £10. But before entries were accepted, evidence of age had to be supplied, as there were many cases of younger people trying to race against the genuine senior citizens. This age-checking process was a very long one.

Can you think of a much more efficient way of dealing with the age checks?

See page 202

Friendly chat

For years, two people used to chat regularly with each other. One day they went to a restaurant. Although they sat face-to-face at the same table, they spoke not a single word to each other, before the meal, during it or afterwards. They had not fallen out, and they spoke to each other again as usual the following day and other days thereafter. Can you explain?

See page 203

Light burden

I entered a room and there were five men inside, all quite free to move about. Having some strength, I could lift four of them off the ground one at a time, but it was impossible for me to lift the fifth, even though he was the lightest of all. What is the explanation?

See page 204

Extra-strength tissues

How can 2 sheets of tissue paper be used to hold a genuine iron barbell weighing 3kg completely off the floor of the gym, for 4 minutes?

See page 205

A helpful shop for shoplifters

Moriarty Junior, the master thief, went into a shop and stole some of its goods. Not only that, but he induced the shop to *willingly* deliver the stolen goods to his door, thereby helping in the theft. How did he bring this about?

See page 199

Visa interviews

Two men, father and son, who lived together in Mirpur, wanted to come to England for a family reunion. They went to the British Embassy in Islamabad, where they were interviewed separately, one just after the other, to make sure they had a valid reason to enter the country.

Strangely, each of them was asked by the interviewing officer how many cows and bulls they had, how many hens and cockerels, and whether there were any chicks. The applicants wondered why the officer was so interested in their animals, in respect of which no visa applications had been made, and which were to remain in Pakistan in the care of a relative.

The immigration officer had a good reason for asking about the animals. What was it?

See page 201

Sock and trouser

An old miser was seen wandering in town with the bottom of just his right trouser leg tucked into his sock. What's the best explanation?

See page 202

Shirt style

The same old miser was seen with his shirt hanging out of his trousers at the back, but always tucked in at the front. What's the best explanation?

See page 203

Levitating tap

Here is a true story. I once saw a tap, without its pipe, suspended in mid-air, with water continuously gushing out of it. How was this possible?

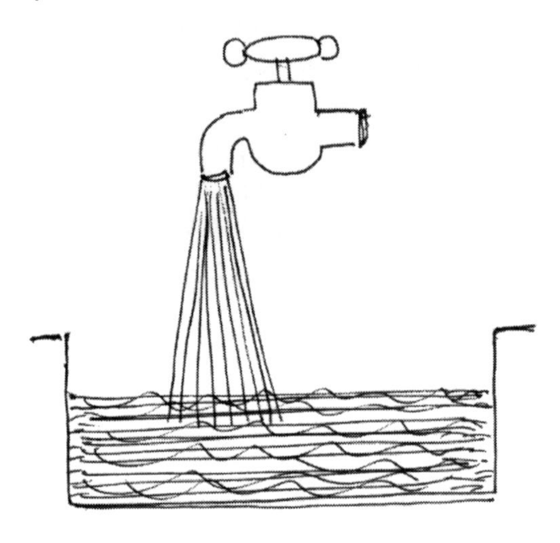

See page 205

Book thief

Moriarty Junior, the master thief, accidentally pays for a book, and is keen to put this matter right. He comes up with an ingenious way of making the bought book a stolen book. He returns to the shop and manages to make the shop assistant *willingly* give the money back for the book, despite keeping it at home. How does he do it?

See page 207

Irrational fear

A man develops a totally irrational fear that the roof of his house is about to fall in on him and his family. Does he consult a GP, psychologist or psychiatrist?

See page 200

Returns policy

You have bought a faulty item from a store, and wish to exchange it. In the case of faulty goods, the store allows a refund or an exchange, but only on presentation of the receipt. Unfortunately you have lost the receipt. What would Moriarty Junior recommend?

See page 201

Monitoring faults

I was pleased to discover that my computer monitor was faulty, even though I had no warranty. Why?

See page 202

Inaudible sound

What kind of ordinary nearby sound is it which one cannot hear, however loud it might get?

See page 204

An incredible crime

There exists a crime, of which it is true to say: the greater the crime, the less the punishment. What is the crime?

See page 207

Answers to Puzzles

Meeting in the forest

The scenario described took place in the carriage of a train going through a forest.

Multi-duty thermometer

By dropping it from the top of the building and recording the time it takes to strike the ground.

Portrait of the author

The author is facing away from the camera, and tilting his face upwards. He has put his clothes on backwards, and put dark glasses on the top of his head – there are no eyes behind them!

A helpful shop for shoplifters

The shop was a Post Office also selling a variety of stationery and other items. Moriarty Junior picked up a number of items that took his fancy, which he then placed into a large padded envelope, also taken off the display. He wrote his name and address on the envelope, took it to the counter and had it posted to himself.

Mirror, mirror

You cannot touch the tip of the index finger you are using! By contrast, this is the *only* part of your reflection that you *can* touch.

I gave a simpler version of this puzzle to Sara, which ran as follows: "What part of your image in the mirror can you touch with your fingertip?" Sara replied, "Anything!" She tried to demonstrate by touching her reflection's ear, but was startled to find that her reflection's finger kept getting in the way.

Breaking the law

You were driving on a fast road and saw a driver coming towards you in the opposite direction, on the wrong side.

Irrational fear

The question was: 'Does he consult a GP, psychologist or psychiatrist?' The answer is No. He consults a builder.

Cook's surprise

My degree of appreciation of her meals over the years had honed her cooking skills to perfection.

Disappearing act

It's a hole (not a balloon, which was Sara's reply).

Epistemological puzzle

I knew the other landscapes of Switzerland extremely well, but Davos was the only place in Switzerland that I hadn't seen. If I didn't recognise the landscape, it had to be Davos. Paradoxically, ignorance was the clue to knowledge!

Clock speed

If you lengthen the hour hand, its tip will trace a larger circle each hour, moving a greater distance in the same time, and will therefore be going faster. So lengthen it until the distance the tip travels is enough for the required speed.

Alternatively, and more easily, you could shorten the minute (or second) hand, until its tip is travelling slow enough.

Spare change

You have to pay £4.19, and your cash totals £5.00. So you'll be left with only £0.81 after buying the magazines and newspapers. The simplest method is to find the smallest number of coins totalling £0.81. Keep these (1 of 50p, 1 of 20p, 1 of 10p, and 1 of 1p) and hand over the rest.

Visa interviews

If the applicants were genuinely father and son living together, their answers would have to agree on these matters.

Returns policy

Buy a replacement, and use its receipt, later on, to obtain a refund on the original faulty item.

Finger strength

My daughter sat on an ordinary swing in the local park. With rhythmic movements of a single finger pushing on the seat, I managed to raise the swing, and therefore raise her, to the required height.

Trading places

The shop was part of a petrol station, and my car was behind his at the pumps.

Coin puzzle

Buy a metal detector.

A total loss

Your total loss was £21 (£1 was your *net* loss).

A race for 65's and over

Allow the race to go ahead without checking any ages. Evidence of age need only be checked as required to verify the eligibility of prize winners.

Sock and trouser

He had a hole in his right trouser pocket, and was catching any money he accidentally put in there.

Monitoring faults

My monitor was looking hazy, and I had mistakenly thought something was wrong with my eyes.

Transportation feat

They were all the pieces of a burst lorry-tyre. I pieced the tyre together again, tied it in position with the string, and was then able to send it rolling down the road, which was on a hill.

Moral problem

He himself was born as the result of that rape.

A pint of milk a day

Because milkmen come so early in the morning, the accepted method of communication with them is to leave a note inside an empty bottle outside your house. Moriarty found a loophole in this system.

At the beginning of the month, he left a note in an empty bottle outside his neighbour's house, saying: 'One extra pint a day, from now on, please.' The milkman would have removed this note, acted upon it, *willingly* brought more milk, and never spoken of it to the resident. And each morning, just after the milkman had gone, Moriarty took the extra pint for himself!

By the time the resident received the bill at the end of the month, Moriarty had quietly moved away.

The lecture effect

He had formulated a question, which he wanted to ask, but he couldn't get up the nerve to do so.

Friendly chat

The two people's regular chats were only on the phone. They had never seen each other before their meal, when they happened to go to the same restaurant and sit at the same table purely by accident.

Shirt style

There was a big hole in the back of his trousers, and another in the front of his shirt! He did not want to spend his money to buy a new set.

Inaudible sound

The sound of one's own snoring.

Tax relief

Tax itself is a business expense that is not eligible for tax relief!

Image quality

We were watching an advert for the new television model on our own TV set. So we were admiring the picture quality of our own TV.

God cannot do certain logically possible tasks

For example:

A: To turn you into a brick.

B: To turn Himself into a brick.

Changing rooms

On that day, a male cleaner had to work in the Women's changing room.

Light burden

There were four men in the room before I entered. So I was the fifth man. I cannot lift myself off the ground, however light I might be!

Phone upgrade

He did what he'd always done when upgrading his children's phones. He bought one new phone and gave it to the oldest child. The old phones were handed down from child to child.

Levitating tap

The mouth of the tap was stuck onto a vertical supporting glass tube. Water was flowing up the tube, out at the top and down over its sides, emerging from the mouth of the tap. The water itself was obscuring the tube.

Awkward shopkeeper

The grumpy shopkeeper can be depended upon to obstruct you in any way he can. To defeat him, you can lure him into obstructing you in a way that allows you to turn the tables on him.

First, put the item being returned on the counter, and say, "I'm afraid I've got to return this. It's faulty." Rummage in your pockets as though you have lost your receipt. Make it an apparently thorough search. Then say, "You don't need the receipt, do you?" All this will tempt him to require you to produce the receipt.

Argue the point with him for a while. Make him certain that you do not have the receipt. You might say, "If it's not in my pockets I must have thrown it away." He will gleefully commit himself to demanding that a receipt be produced.

After a while, suddenly think to look in your back pocket, where you are surprised, so surprised, to find the required proof of purchase. The shopkeeper, now fully committed, has no option but to issue a refund!

Extra-strength tissues

Place the 2 tissues on the floor, and then roll the barbell on top of them. They could have supported any weight at all, and for any length of time. The tissues cannot be squeezed out of existence.

Proof that the Earth is stationary

The author was ignorant of the relative sizes of our solar system and the Pole Star. Even though the Pole Star appears to be a dot from Earth, it is in fact as large as our whole solar system!

The South-North axis of the Earth points to the Pole Star, and because this axis has roughly the same orientation throughout the year, it continues to point at the Pole Star. The lateral movement of the Earth is insignificant because of the hugeness of the Pole Star.

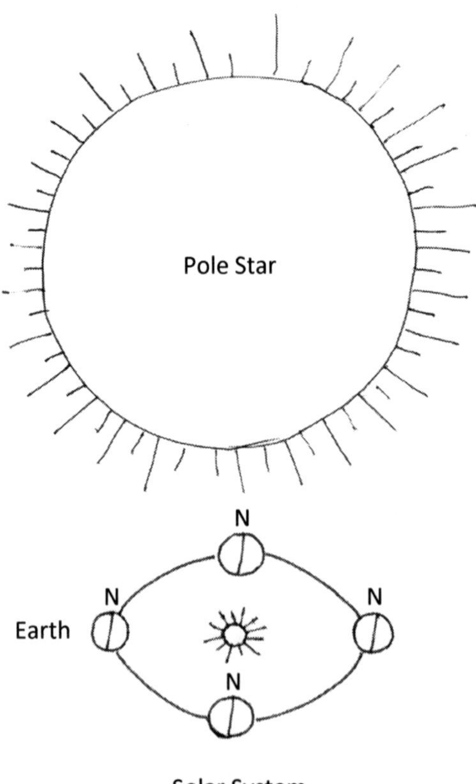

Solar System

Book thief

He takes the receipt back to the shop after a few days, hands it in to customer service, together with another copy of the same book, taken from the shelves, and asks for a refund. He simply has to say that he has changed his mind.

Counting without counting

The objects were the pieces of a complete 120-piece jigsaw puzzle. He did the puzzle.

After giving this solution to my friend Richard, he came up with an even better one which would have allowed the innumerate man to count the objects no matter what they were. If the man had read Bertrand Russell's *The Principles of Mathematics*, he would know that performing a simple one-to-one correspondence between the objects and his own 120-piece jigsaw at home would do the trick.

An incredible crime

I am afraid I have forgotten the answer to this puzzle!

However, discerning readers will be able to realise that my memory lapse has deprived them of nothing that they might have expected in the first place. Why should this be so?

See www.mahmudkhan.com/moustache/answer

Epilogue

"Man is but a reed, the most feeble thing in nature, but he is a thinking reed."

Blaise Pascal

Meditation on humility

The Universe has been here for some fifteen billion years without us. It could very well have carried on for all eternity without us. And when humanity is no more, the Universe will carry on, perhaps inexorably, in our absence. It doesn't depend on us for its existence, but we certainly depend on it. Our coming into existence was so unlikely that we are lucky to exist at all.

And now that we find ourselves here, existing, how do we spend our time? We compete with each other for the making of material gains, for acquiring more money, more land, more property. Initially, we are interested in money only as a means to achieving our other desired ends. But the distinction between means and ends often becomes so blurred that we begin to see money as an end in itself. The avaricious and miserly should consider this: at the time of your death, your leftover bank balance represents what can only be described as voluntary work on your part – though, ironically, done involuntarily!

We sometimes become so dominated by worldly pursuits and the struggle for a better life that we forget to look at the question of what really matters. Surely, life is not all about money, land and property? Health and happiness, love and friendship, justice and fair play, compassion, works of art and music seem to make better candidates for worthwhile pursuits.

Regardless of what we do, all our good and evil deeds will eventually submerge in the ocean of time. There will come a time when even those who remembered those who remembered us will be long dead. Will anything matter to you in this bleak time after your death? Could anything matter at all when just the Universe remains, and life is no more?

Some philosophers think that whatever meaning we succeed in giving to life is within life itself, not beyond it. Everything that matters lies between the two most significant events of our lives: our birth and our death. But the passage between these two milestones is truly baffling. Sometimes I find that one TV channel is showing an old Indian film where the haughty hero Shammi Kapoor is robust, rubicund and in the prime of life, while another channel is showing him in a recent film in which he is a frail old man. Whenever a child is born and comes home, an old person somewhere else dies and is taken to a graveyard. In my mind's eye, I can see one as the future of the other!

Our birth represents vulnerability, dependency, and obscurity surrounding our origin. Our death, on the other hand, represents certainty – the inevitable and eternal loss of everything. Death is the most absolute form of loss. It dispossesses us of all things, leaving us in the poverty of inheriting at most 6 foot by 2 foot of land. All things gained in life cease to remain our own after death.

The death of a loved one changes the whole course of a person's life. It makes some people religious, some philosophical, some stronger, some weaker. It reveals our helplessness before the Universe – which doesn't care, and grinds on, uninterested.

I find life utterly mysterious – more mysterious indeed than anything else in the Universe. The cosmologist Sir Martin Rees once said that even a frog is much more fascinating, complex and mystifying than the Sun!

What are we? We come into this world regardless of whether we are welcomed or not. Our parents, whom we could not choose, made an original contribution of a tiny amount of matter in order to lay our foundations, and ever since then we have been borrowing matter from the Universe and paying it back. And we make our final repayment to the Universe when we die. Perhaps this is what is meant by the phrase 'ashes to ashes, dust to dust'.

Two places can help us all, young and old, to put things into perspective, and to remind us of our humble origin and inevitable end. The two places I have in mind are maternity units and graveyards. It is important sometimes to visit these places to help us meditate on life, and on death.

These two places conjure some deep philosophical questions. What is the point of life? Is the struggle with each other for supremacy and worldly gains only an exercise in futility? Is life to be regarded as absurd and frivolous, or serious? Is the purpose of life merely to kill time before time kills you? Or is our life nothing more than just a journey from a maternity unit to a graveyard – where, whatever happens in between, we all become equal in **the end**?

Lightning Source UK Ltd.
Milton Keynes UK
13 May 2010

154127UK00002B/183/P